TWELVE HOURS TO DESTINY

At the height of the Cold War one of the most trusted and important British agents in Hong Kong, Chao Lin, suddenly vanishes, and in London Steve Carradine is put on the case. Now hints are filtering through to Hong Kong of a new weapon with which the Chinese hope to dominate the world, and Chao Lin is the only man outside of China to possess this vital information. Carradine's assignment is simple: Find Chao Lin, discover the nature of this secret weapon, and bring both out of China!

MANNING K. ROBERTSON

TWELVE HOURS TO DESTINY

Complete and Unabridged

LINFORD
Leicester

First published in Great Britain in 1967

First Linford Edition
published 2015

A catalogue record for this book is available
from the British Library.

ISBN 978–1–4448–2448–3

1

The Night Brings Danger

The sun, which had hovered almost interminably above the hills on the Chinese mainland, vanished abruptly in a sweeping of red and orange. The day ended as far as the sea and the wharves which stretched around most of Hong Kong island were concerned. But up on the crown of Victoria Peak, daylight still lingered as though reluctant to give way to the swiftly advancing night.

Along the wide, steep steps of Sing Wong Street looking down over the harbour, there was the usual late evening activity: coolies from the waterfront rubbing shoulders with high-class Chinese and Europeans. Within an hour the street would become deserted, lying as it did between the dives and hovels of the downtown area and the highly residential district on the slopes of Victoria Peak. At this time of the day the long, straight street was cool and seemingly detached from the rest of the sprawling city with the tall offices of rich businessmen on either side, their owners closing up for the day. The occasional bright brass plate bearing the title of a holding company in Great Britain or Australia was usually genuine; but here and there were others which were not quite what they appeared on the surface.

On the second floor of one of the tall buildings were the offices of Chao Lin, dealer in textile fibres, yarns and fabrics. Well-known in Hong Kong, and respected by his associates, he was a man of strict behaviour. Every working day of the week he would leave the building at precisely six fifteen and make his way down Sing Wong Street to where a car would be waiting to take him home; every day except Fridays, when his office would be the only one along that stretch of the street still showing a light and when he would remain there for more than three hours after the rest of the business people had left for their evening pleasures.

During normal business hours, any

visitor to the address would be shown into a respectable, well-appointed room typical of such places in this sector of Hong Kong, with several typists seated at long desks, busy telephones, tall dark-green metal filing cabinets and all the usual accoutrements of a high-class business centre. If one were a very important client, one might be shown through — by an efficient Chinese secretary — into Chao Lin's inner sanctum where tea would be provided in tiny eggshell-thin porcelain cups while details of shipments would be discreetly discussed.

Nothing seen by the many visitors to the office would give the impression that anything more went on there than the normal day-to-day business of running an efficient import and export company dealing in one of Hong Kong's expanding trades with the Western world. Only at six thirty each Friday evening was the procedure changed, after all of the office staff had left. Then Chao Lin would press a concealed button beneath his desk and a square section of the far wall, ostensibly a large filing cabinet, would turn with an oiled smoothness on a central pivot, revealing an entrance to the small room whose existence was known to only a handful of trusted men in London and Hong Kong.

At precisely seven o'clock, Hong Kong time, he would be seated before the powerful transmitter, earphones clamped tightly over his head, listening intently for the call sign from London which would link him with a desk at the headquarters of British Military Intelligence. Once the signal came through, he would dispatch all of his carefully gathered information for the week in a business-like and concise manner, vital information which had been gathered, in the main, from a patient monitoring of Chinese radio broadcasts; for since China had been closed to all but a few special visitors from the West, a ring of listening posts had been set up by Western Intelligence to monitor every programme broadcast inside Communist China.

Already this procedure had paid handsome dividends. Since Russia had stopped the all-important supply of ground-to-air missiles, American U2 spy planes had been able to fly virtually unhindered over the Chinese mainland. Satellites, too, made passes over China, photographing and recording the presence of nuclear factories in Sinkiang Province at Lop Nor close to the Russian frontier. This information, coupled with broadcasts describing the building of new roads in that area, roads which had been laid across the Sinkiang Desert, gave the clue to the construction of the first Chinese atomic bomb long before it had been tested.

Now there was a hint of something as dramatic going on inside China: little scattered bits of information which Chao Lin had picked up from various sources and from which he was in the process of building up an overall picture which indicated something really big. It might require some weeks of patient work to fill in all of the blanks, but he was a patient man and London would wait until he could give them everything they needed.

On this particular Friday evening, Chao Lin moved purposefully around the outer room of the office, checking that everything was in order. The last of the employees had gone and the place was deathly quiet. He glanced at the watch on his left wrist. Another thirty-five minutes and the call sign from London would be beaming its way through the ether. Locking the outer door, he made his way through into the back room.

★   ★   ★

At the same moment that the steel bolt on Chao Lin's outer office shot home, the high-pitched whine of the engines of the small submarine faded to a low-throated moan and then fell silent. There was a slight, scarcely-felt jar throughout the whole metal structure as the craft touched bottom. The two men in gleaming black skin-tight suits and aqualungs moved slowly towards the escape hatch. Behind the transparent masks, their faces were inscrutable, narrowed eyes and watchful, fixed on the olive features of Commander Chi ten Lao.

'You have your instructions.' The commander's tone was soft but had an urgent edge to it. 'We are now in fifty feet

6

of water some four hundred yards outside the harbour at Hong Kong. Once you leave through the escape hatch, you will make your way underwater to the harbour and rendezvous with the junk having the red sail. There is no possibility of a mistake. There you will change your clothing and make your way onshore to the address you have been given in Sing Wong Street. Once you arrive at the house and offices of Chao Lin, you will carry out phase two of the plan. This is perfectly understood.' The final sentence was a statement of fact and not a question.

The two men nodded slowly in agreement. It would have been strange had they not done so. Each man had been carefully chosen for this task; had been briefed with a thoroughness which was peculiar to the Chinese. It was, indeed, a mark of the utter importance of their mission that one of the few submarines possessed by the Chinese had been used to bring them to the spot from a secluded point on the mainland.

Chi ten Lao was silent for a long

minute. Then he nodded slowly. 'I am satisfied,' he murmured finally. Turning, he gave a brief signal to the men standing on either side of the steel door leading to the escape hatch. They spun the great wheel that operated the mechanism, waited until both men had passed through into the narrow chamber beyond, then closed the heavy steel door behind them. Unconcernedly, the commander returned to his post. His job was almost finished for the time being. For Yun Shih-Min and Chu Hsi it was just beginning.

Savagely the blast of compressed air caught Chu Hsi around in the middle and hurled him upward through the dark water. The surface of the sea still high above him was also dark; featureless. He commenced to swim to one side as a further ballooning of bubbles shot from the black whale-like shape of the submarine below him and Yun Shih-Min was projected upward, gliding beside him a few moments later. Together, they swam some twenty feet below the surface to obtain decompression.

Breaking surface three minutes later,

the two dark shapes slid easily through the waves to where the tall cranes and gantries of Hong Kong Harbour lay on the dim skyline. Off to their left, a small cluster of junks bobbed up and down in the water. When they were less than fifty yards away they paused, treading water to keep themselves upright, scanning the long line of small vessels until they were able to pick out one a short distance from the others, the red square sail standing out prominently in the dim starlight. Chu Hsi pointed, then dipped his right hand downward to indicate that they would swim the rest of the way underwater so as not to leave any tell-tale wake which might be seen from the other fishing vessels in the vicinity. Everything depended on the utmost secrecy. The British authorities had eyes everywhere — though they were on the lookout for smugglers rather than swimmers moving in from the ocean.

Just for a moment, before submerging, he wondered why Lung Shan wanted Chao Lin so desperately that he had devised this method of getting him out of Hong Kong. As a small cog in a very large and complex machine, he did not ask questions of those in authority and simply carried out the orders given to him. All that really mattered was his ultimate success in this particular mission. If he and his companion delivered Chao Lin to Lung Chan all would be well; if not . . . He immediately put any thought of failure out of his mind. Lung Chan was the Devil incarnate. If he wanted Chao Lin — and alive — then it was for some purpose which he, Chu Hsi, did not wish to contemplate.

They broke surface again less than ten yards from the junk. There were three men on board to help them over the side. Fresh clothing was waiting for them. Now it was only a question of speed: of relying on the precision with which everything had been planned in advance.

At exactly six fifty, with the swiftly rising length of Sing Wong Street standing virtually deserted before them, the two men walked unhurriedly up the wide steps. There was a strict professionalism about the way they forced the lock of the outer door and slipped noiselessly inside.

Crossing the room, they moved towards a far door and paused, listening intently. No sound came from the other side, but a faint slip of yellow light showed plainly from beneath the door . . .

Gently, Chao Lin eased himself forward in his chair, taking up the most comfortable position. A quick glance at his watch told him that London should be coming through any second now. Everything was in readiness. Inside the small room there was no sound beyond the faint humming of the powerful transmitter with its neat rows of dials and flickering needles. His fingertips brushed the dial in front of him.

Right hand poised above the gleaming transmitter key, he waited patiently for the slight change in the modulated note which would warn him that the code signal was coming through over the ether.

The first he knew that there was something wrong was the hard, deadly touch of cold steel against his temple just above the left ear. Almost automatically, without thinking, he dropped his hand away from the key and swung it sharply

11

across his body to where the tiny automatic reposed in the holster under his left armpit, his whole body swivelling in the chair.

Something struck him hard across the wrist, smashing the bones in an agonising stab of pain. The gun dropped with a clatter to the floor at his feet and he twisted his head with a wrenching of neck muscles, staring up at the two men who stood menacingly over him.

'You are a fool, Chao Lin,' said the taller of the men contemptuously.

'Who are you?'

'That is of no importance. All that matters is that we know who you are.'

The small black hole of the gun with the ugly cylinder of the silencer screwed over the barrel was aimed straight at his eyes. For a moment, as he heard the faint staccato click of the call sign in the earphones, he debated whether to send a warning signal, even though it would almost certainly be his last action on this earth. Then he shrugged resignedly. He had made up his mind. He had no other alternative. The fact that these men had

12

known who he was, and where to find him, was enough to know that he did not have a chance of warning London that there was something wrong. Perhaps when he did not acknowledge their signal, they would put two and two together and realise that something was gravely wrong.

Weakly, he let his right hand drop to his lap. One of the men picked up the fallen automatic and thrust it into his belt. The other tugged the earphones off his head, held them against his ear for a moment, then smiled thinly and tossed them contemptuously onto the shelf in front of the transmitter.

'You will send no more messages of any kind to your imperialistic masters, old man.' The other backed away a little. 'Get up. Move very slowly or we shall kill you.'

Feebly, trying to shut out of his mind the searing flame of agony that lanced through his broken wrist, stabbing through the whole length of his arm, Chao Lin got up out of the chair. The short, stocky one of the pair pushed him towards the door, waited until he was just inside the other room, then swung downward with his left

13

hand, fingers stiffened. The edge of his palm caught Chao Lin on the back of the neck. With a sigh, the other collapsed forward, unconscious even before his inert body hit the floor. Chao Lin did not even feel the jarring pain as his injured wrist crumpled under his weight.

In the small back room, Chu Hsi smashed the flimsy wooden chair to bits using the unyielding side of the transmitter, then proceeded to wreck the rest of the furniture, piling it high against one wall. Finally, he tore down the silk curtains with their red and gold printed designs, thrust them into the pile, struck a couple of matches and waited until the wood was well ablaze before joining Yun Shih-Min. He nodded tersely. Calmly, the other bent, heaved the limp body over his shoulder and followed him to the outer door. Behind them, the first wisps of grey smoke were oozing through the concealed door into the room.

Twenty minutes later, a junk with a red sail drifted slowly and inconspicuously from the others which bobbed at their moorings and moved out into the stretch of water between Hong Kong and the Chinese mainland. Standing in the bow, Chu Hsi scanned the dark, heaving waters. Overhead, the diamond-hard stars glittered brilliantly, but he had no eyes for them. These waters were, he knew, constantly patrolled by the British Navy, on the lookout for opium smugglers, and they were liable to stop, board and search any small vessel behaving in a peculiar manner. In the event of this happening before they rendezvoused with the submarine, it would be necessary for them to put their emergency plan into operation.

Outwardly, the junk looked no different from the thousands of others which milled back and forth in Hong Kong Harbour, but there was one very vital difference. To a practised eye, it would be seen that the vessel lay very low in the water at the bow. But it was utterly out of the question that the British, even if this were noted, would guess at the reason for it. The *reason* was the heavy, recoilless 4.5-inch gun which lay concealed within the bows — a weapon quite capable of blowing a British torpedo boat out of the water with a couple of well-aimed shots.

There was an urgent touch on his arm. Yun Shih-Min pointed out to sea. Narrowing his eyes, Chu Hsi glimpsed the creaming of white bow foam out in the clear channel. The torpedo boat was coming up fast, driven under the full power of her mighty engines.

'Warn the gunners to stand by,' he ordered crisply. There was no emotion in his voice.

The creaming bow wave died away to a faint ripple of phosphorescence, the throb of the powerful diesel dying away to a muted murmur as the British boat moved towards him, scarcely more than a hundred yards away now. Chu Hsi saw the gunners standing by on the deck and saw the two officers relaxed near the bow, but not too relaxed. They were prepared for trouble. One of the officers cupped his hands and yelled to them in halting Chinese. It was an order to lower their sail and prepare to be bordered.

Chu Hsi hesitated for only a fraction of a second, then signalled sharply with his right hand. He knew that the small square hatch covering the muzzle of the gun had been removed some ten seconds before, ready for his signal.

Suddenly, from just below the bow of the junk, a red-tipped bolt of flame and smoke lanced out. The sound came a split second later, to be followed by the explosion as the heavy shell smashed into the midships of the torpedo boat. Instinctively, Chu Hsi had hurled himself to the deck. Two more shells followed in rapid succession. From that range, it was utterly impossible to miss. The men on board the British boat died literally without knowing that anything was wrong. The deep echoes faded gradually over the sea. Bits of debris clattered onto the deck of the junk as Chu Hsi pushed himself to his feet. The torpedo boat was going down, sinking fast. She was heavily on fire amidships but the explosions had evidently smashed the bottom out of her and fifteen seconds later, the vessel canted sharply to starboard and slid beneath the surface in a hissing steam, as the fuel tanks erupted just beneath the water.

Twenty minutes later, and two miles further offshore, the sleek shape of the waiting submarine nosed out of the water and the junk was manoeuvred alongside. Chao Lin was stirring into consciousness as he was picked up and lifted on board.

★ ★ ★

Leaning sideways in his seat, Commander Steve Carradine peered through the small square window and watched the filmy clouds reach up and envelop the Viscount as they began to reduce height. The stewardess paused beside his seat, glanced archly down at him.

'Would you fasten your seatbelt, sir.'

Carradine grinned and nodded. Deftly, he clicked the belt shut around his waist and leaned back. The plane lurched momentarily as they hit an air pocket and the note of the engines changed abruptly for a second. The grin stayed on his lips as he watched the girl swaying along the aisle towards the pilot's cabin, but inwardly, his stomach was in turmoil. There were only two things he disliked about their travel: taking off and getting down again. The bit in the middle seldom troubled him; he could somehow manage to forget that he was suspended several thousand feet above solid ground in a steel shell and withdraw his mind into a small private world. The clouds thinned and he was able to see the chequered fields and lacing roads and then, somewhere ahead, the wide criss-cross of the runways of London airport, with the toy-like control tower a little to one side.

He let his breath go from between his teeth and wished that the red NO SMOKING sign was not showing above the interconnecting door. The Viscount put its sleek nose down towards the distant runway. The shrill whine of the engines deepened. There was a rush of air past the wings and fuselage. Then they were skimming over the countryside. He glimpsed roads and houses just beneath him, then the concrete lane of the runway almost on the same level as the window. A bump as the undercarriage wheels touched, a pause and then a further jar. The plane wobbled slightly, then steadied as they touched down.

As he waited for customs clearance, Carradine tried to figure out why his vacation in southern France should have been so abruptly ended — why his presence was needed so urgently here in London. God knew his idyllic spells were few and far between. It just wasn't fair for them to be interrupted in this way.

'All right, Mr. Carradine. You're clear to go through.' The customs officer nodded across at him, scribbled some unintelligible marking chalk on his two cases and slid them along the counter. He said something to his companion in a low undertone as Carradine picked them up and walked away. Glancing over his shoulder, he saw their curious gaze fixed on him. Shrugging, he left the building, noticing at once the tall man who came in his direction. There was a car parked at the kerb having the nondescript look he always associated with any of the cars used by Military Intelligence.

'I'm to take you direct to Headquarters, sir.' The other took his cases and thrust them into the spacious boot.

Carradine settled himself into the seat, grateful for the space which allowed him to stretch his legs out to the full.

When they were moving smoothly into the stream of traffic, the driver said politely: 'Not the best of weather to have to come back to, sir.'

Carradine gave a brief nod. The beating rain which slashed at the windscreens defied the moving fingers of the wipers to do their damnedest to clear it away. The warm, mellow sun of south of France seemed an eternity away at that moment. 'I've known better,' he answered morosely.

★   ★   ★

There was no sound sound in the large room on the fifth floor of the tall building, although the rain and wind still beat down against the glass of the shuttered windows. Carradine met the gaze of the man seated at the desk, noticing the stillness of the face, the coldness in the eyes.

Something was worrying the old man immensely, he decided. It was seldom he had seen him as preoccupied as this. The other said in a deceptively soft tone: 'Sorry to have to recall you in this abrupt way.' He sat back, resting his hands flat on top of the desk. His tone belied the feeling behind his statement. 'You ready to go back to work right away?'

'Why yes, sir.' Carradine nodded. What was coming now? he wondered tensely. More trouble in some obscure corner of the world? Or a humdrum desk job here in the heart of London where nothing ever happened to break the monotony?

'Good.' The other's tone became abruptly businesslike. He pulled the solitary folder towards him and flipped back the stiff cover. Carradine saw that it had been marked with a single red star, indicating that the contents were top secret. The Chief tapped the folder significantly with his forefinger.

'I'm expecting the Chief of Staff here in five minutes, but before he arrives, I want to put you in the picture as far as this affair is concerned. Our top agent in Hong Kong is a man by the name of Chao Lin. Ostensibly, he heads an export-import business dealing in fabrics. Contact is made with him every Friday night at nineteen hours Hong Kong time. A week ago he failed to acknowledge our call sign and all attempts to raise him have failed.'

'There could be an innocent explanation,' Carradine suggested.

'I doubt it.' The Chief shook his head emphatically. 'There was no indication from his last message that anything was wrong.'

'What kind of man was he, sir?'

'Extremely conscientious. He was the man who passed on that information about activities around Sinkiang which put us on to their atomic tests. It seems he had discovered something else, something pretty big. He was looking into it and was supposed to send on anything he found as soon as possible.'

'So naturally you suspect that the Communists got on to him first?'

'In a single word — yes. In this job, you get the smell of a thing in your nostrils. This smells bad. As of now, we're opening a file on Chao Lin. You are assigned to this case. I want you to — ' He broke off as a buzzer sounded on his desk and the red light over the door went on. 'That will be the Chief of Staff.'

The other came in a moment later and gave Carradine a brief, friendly nod. Carradine had worked with him on several occasions in the past and knew the tall grey-haired man intimately. Apart from the Chief himself, Benton possibly knew more about the running of Headquarters than anyone else. He was an extremely able man whose rigid military training showed in his erect bearing. Carradine had the impression that at times the other would have willingly exchanged the endless grind of paperwork and responsibility for the kind of life which he himself led.

'Take a pew,' said the Chief, nodding towards a chair. 'I'm assigning Carradine to the Hong Kong case. A funny affair to say the best of it.'

'I agree.' Benton glanced sideways at Carradine. 'There's something really big going on in that part of the world and it's essential that we find out what it is. Chao Lin put us on to the fact that the Chinese were preparing to explode their first nuclear weapon. He's one of our shrewdest men, not the kind likely to have flights of fancy as some of our men are.'

'You've no idea at all what it might be?' Carradine addressed the question to both of them. 'A hydrogen bomb, perhaps?'

'It could be,' agreed Benton, lips pursed into a tight line. 'Although somehow I doubt it. The construction of such a weapon would be a logical outcome of the experiments we know they're carrying out. No, I'm positive this is something of a different nature.'

'In the last message but one, he mentioned that there were hints the Chinese were working on a secret weapon.' The Chief's voice was tightly controlled. 'Whatever it is that is going on in the enemy camp, we must have information on it as soon as possible. I understand that you underwent an intensive course in Chinese two years ago. How did it turn out?'

'It isn't a language you pick up very readily,' Carradine said, a trifle defensively. 'Not like Russian.'

'I realise that you are perfectly fluent in Russian,' said the Chief testily. 'I'm interested at the moment in whether you can speak and understand sufficient Chinese to enable you to pass as one.'

'No.' Carradine shook his head decisively. 'I doubt if there are more than a handful of Westerners who do.'

'That is the answer I expected.' The other showed no sign of surprise. 'It's therefore quite obvious you will need a cover when you go there and unfortunately that is not going to be easy.' He stared sombrely at Carradine. His face was grim.

'Look,' Carradine begged. 'I'm completely lost at the moment. If I'm merely to discover what has happened to Chao Lin and try to unearth the information he stumbled on, I shall presumably be operating inside Hong Kong and surely I can — '

'You're wrong,' interrupted the other harshly. 'That isn't what you're to do at all. Hong Kong will merely be your jumping-off point. All of the evidence points to Chao Lin having been kidnapped and taken by junk, or submarine, to China. That will be your ultimate objective. To find where Chao Lin is being held and get him back, together with this vital information he has, and also carry out any further actions you may think fit.'

So that was it! That was the reason he had been recalled so abruptly from his holiday in the south of France.

Before he could say anything further, Benton chimed in with: 'You may be wondering how we can be so sure that Chao Lin is now inside Communist China. The brief answer is that on the same evening as Chao Lin was scheduled to contact us as usual, one of our torpedo boats patrolling the waters off Hong Kong Harbour was attacked and sunk by a Chinese junk.'

'By a junk?'

'Exactly. Not the sort of thing one would expect to happen. But there was one survivor from the torpedo boat. He was picked up two hours later, clinging to a piece of driftwood, more dead than alive. We had him flown back to England as soon as he was well enough to be moved. You interrogated him, Benton. You can tell Carradine his story better than I.'

Benton sat forward on the edge of his chair. 'There isn't much to tell,' he began. 'Apparently this junk was sighted heading away from the harbour just after dark, acting in a highly suspicious manner. Naturally, it was thought they were dope smugglers. There's been plenty of that going on in the past few years. Just a routine search, they thought. What they hadn't bargained for was a concealed heavy-calibre gun in the bow of the junk. It took only three shells to sink the torpedo boat within minutes. They never had a chance to fight back.'

'Good Lord.' Carradine tried to keep the surprise out of his voice. 'So they really mean business.'

'That is an understatement. Somehow, they must have tumbled to Chao Lin. The fact that all of this must have been planned in advance with the precision of a military mission gives us an indication of how seriously they took him as a threat to their security. Evidently they had to get him out of Hong Kong without anyone knowing. Thousands of men vanish

28

without trace from Hong Kong and no one bothers about it. As far as the authorities there are concerned, one man is just another of those faceless thousands. We shall, of course, let them continue to think that way.'

Carradine sat back in his chair and regarded the other thoughtfully. 'I assume that this man, Chao Lin, was working alone?'

'No.' The Chief shook his head. 'He had a Number Two working with him. Man by the name of Kellaway. Wing-Commander in the Fighter Command before he came over to us. A good man in every respect.'

'And where is he now?'

'Still in Hong Kong. We considered it best not to pull him out yet. That decision may be forced on us soon, unless you manage to turn up something definite.'

'When you say he's a good man, I presume that means he can be trusted?'

The Chief shot him an enigmatic glance. 'We did take into account that possibility,' he murmured, as though reading Carradine's mind. 'It's quite evident that there has been a leak somewhere and naturally Kellaway was the first choice as suspect. Nothing is against him according to his confidential record. Something of a ladies' man, but nothing else which would explain him going over to the enemy camp.'

Carradine shrugged. 'I might get in contact with him when I arrive. If he can be trusted it would give me a start.'

'Very well. But keep your eyes and ears open. Give him the file, Benton. I want you to go through it and commit it all to memory. By rights, you would need some weeks of training and preparation. Unfortunately, the affairs of the world won't allow that. I want you out there as soon as possible. All of the arrangements to get you to Hong Kong will be made here but once there, it will be entirely up to you how you proceed. Naturally, you won't be able to go into China as an Englishman. The detailed execution of the mission will be in your hands.' He paused, then: 'By the way, which Chinese dialect did you study during the course?'

'Cantonese,' Carradine replied.

'Good.' The other's eyes gleamed. 'This is evidently going to be the most difficult assignment you have been given so far. How you'll pass as a Chinese Communist, I don't know. The only consolation you have is that if you fail, no one will be able to help you.' Dryly, he added: 'Perhaps that fact alone will put you on your mettle to succeed.'

'Yes, sir.' Carradine knew not to ask any further questions. He had been given all the information available. Picking up the dossier which Benton slid towards him, he walked over to the door. The two men seated at the desk were talking together in low voices. They did not look up as Carradine went out and closed the door quietly behind him.

The Chief said softly: 'What do you consider his chances are, Benton?'

'I'm a little worried about this man Kellaway. If he is reliable, then Carradine may get through without too much difficulty. But if he is the link with the Communists, then he's headed into big trouble.'

'He's been with us for almost fifteen

years now. In all that time there hasn't been a breath of suspicion concerning him. Chao Lin seemed convinced he was reliable. On the other hand, do we have any other alternative but to trust him? He's the only man we have in that part of the world who can give any help to Carradine.'

'Yet someone must have given information to the Chinese,' pointed out the other shrewdly. 'They're not mind-readers any more than we are and the way they carried out Chao Lin's kidnapping is sure proof that they knew every little detail about him. If the operator is correct and the radio link with Chao Lin was open, then they must have struck just at the moment that he was preparing to come on to the air. How could they have known that unless they had been given every last bit of information about him from someone he trusted implicitly?'

It was a question to which there could be no answer.

2

Dawn Like Thunder

Once again, Carradine was nearing the end of a journey. The plane which had carried him from London Airport on a rainy, misty day now droned self-consciously high above the clouds somewhere en route from Bangkok to Hong Kong. The brief stay at Bangkok had been sufficient to chase away the wet dreariness of England and had given him a taste of the tropics. Now, glancing out of the window at the deep blueness of the sea below him, he attempted to think of the mission which lay ahead and already the tense tingle of anticipatory excitement was beginning to curl up inside him, like an icy finger running up and down the inside of his stomach and chest. On the rack immediately above his head was the tiny case which had been specially made up for him by the Special Branch of intelligence. By now, he was used to their efforts to make certain that he had the latest weapons in his armoury; not that he often used them, preferring the heavy Luger pistol which reposed in a shoulder holster.

The plane which he had boarded at Bangkok for this last leg of his journey was perhaps the oldest that BOAC still had flying anywhere in the world. On this particular trip it was flying with only half a dozen oddly assorted passengers on board. Leaning back, Carradine studied them from beneath lowered lids: a couple of wealthy Chinese, a tall, good-looking black African man, and two Europeans apart from himself.

The previous day, he had finished with the folder on the Chao Lin case and handed it back to Benton. There had been relatively little in it that he hadn't learned during the brief interview when he had been assigned to this case and the paucity of information was one of the main causes of his uneasiness. He disliked going into anything of this nature knowing so little about what to expect or how he was to go about his mission. Sitting forward in his seat, he sifted the smallest details of Chao Lin's disappearance through his mind, trying to find the key to the mystery which was drawing nearer to him at more than three hundred miles every hour.

The plane banked slightly, changing course, now heading north-eastward. Here, the day was almost ended. There was a pale sickle of a moon showing through the window, but the sun was still above the horizon somewhere behind them, although down below, the smooth waters were half in shadow. He remembered that up here, above the rose-tinted clouds, they would remain in sunlight longer than anyone on the ground.

There was only another fifty minutes before they were scheduled to arrive at the airport on the mainland across from Hong Kong Island. He began putting his thoughts in order, dragging them back to the present. He had already decided that he would need to get in touch with Kellaway as soon as possible unless arrangements had already been made for the other to meet him.

The stewardess brought him a whisky

and he sat back enjoying the drink because it took his mind temporarily off his trouble. By the time he had finished it, they were already slanting downward through the clear late-evening air towards Hong Kong Airport some four miles from Kowloon.

The lights of Hong Kong Island showed clearly across the mile-wide channel which lay between Victoria and the mainland, spangling the area around the waterfront and sneaking up the side of Victoria Peak. Then there was no time to watch the scene outside with such interest for a slight jar indicated that the undercarriage was down and locked in position and the air began to shrill as the brakes extended from the trailing edges of the wings and they began the long glide over the sea towards the distant runway.

Minutes later, the plane wheeled to a stop before the modern buildings of Hong Kong Airport, rivalling any that Carradine had ever seen. He climbed slowly down the ladder which had been wheeled into position and together with the handful of passengers made his way towards the customs shed. Most of the men were Chinese, he noticed — keen-eyed men who examined everything with a perfunctory attention to detail. The small case which had been made up specially for him passed muster as he had expected. The licence he had for the Luger was scanned thoughtfully, then handed back to him. He had expected awkward questions to be asked concerning the gun. Even here, in this part of the world, bringing in the heavy pistols was frowned upon by the authorities, but there were no questions to be answered, nothing but a polite scrutiny before he was passed through. He had time to notice that at least two of his fellow passengers were receiving far less favoured treatment, and time to ponder briefly on it, before he was out of the building, looking about him in the clear, calm night.

'Carradine?' said a quiet voice at his elbow.

He turned sharply, then relaxed. 'You could only be Kellaway,' he said off-handedly. 'Only you would know I was due to arrive.'

'Right first time, old man.' The other grinned. Carradine felt a little irritated by the man's manner, but fought the feeling down. He knew the type instantly. Public school. Service with the RAF in which he would soon rise to a position of authority and then, probably finding peacetime service too dull, too routine, he had come to Intelligence hoping for a life of adventure and instead, had found himself posted out here where, in spite of the exotic surroundings, life was far from exciting and one day was very much like the rest. Such a humdrum life, for a man searching for high adventure, could be a reason for going over to the enemy camp and playing a double game.

'I wasn't sure whether anyone would be here to meet me or not.'

The other nodded noncommittally. 'The Chief thought it best that I should be here to pick you up. Since we lost Chao Lin, we can't afford to take any chances.'

While he had been speaking, the other had taken Carradine's cases, except for the small one which Carradine insisted politely on carrying himself, and led the way towards a car which waited for them just outside the terminal buildings.

Sliding into the seat, Carradine glanced obliquely at the other as Kellaway crushed into the driver's seat after depositing the cases in the back. Had there been something a little out of place in the other's tone, as if the man were being continually on the defensive? he wondered. Perhaps he was being a little hard on the other. After all, the entire Intelligence station here in Hong Kong had been disrupted; put out of action by the enemy.

Kellaway twisted the ignition key. The engine roared into life. Then they were shooting away from the kerb and cutting along the road towards Kowloon.

'How did it happen?' Carradine sat back, still watchful.

'You mean about Chao Lin? I only wish to God I knew. I wasn't there at the time. He was a very careful man. Said we were not to be seen together unless it was absolutely necessary. We used to meet three times a week on the outskirts of Victoria, usually down near the docks. I'd give him all of the information I'd managed to pick up and he would put me in the picture as far as his side of the business was concerned.'

'Wasn't that an odd way of doing business? As his Number Two, surely you knew virtually everything he was doing?'

'That's how I thought it was supposed to be,' said the other harshly. 'But he said that there were too many people watching Europeans and that working for the Hong Kong station was different from any other. He may have been right. After all there are more than three and a half million Chinese in Hong Kong and only a few thousand Europeans. They run the place in spite of what people might think in London.'

'Then you've no idea at all what happened that night?'

'Only that whoever did it made a dammed good job of destroying the station. The entire place was gutted. All of the records were destroyed, together with the transmitter.' The other paused, then went on: 'You know about the torpedo boat?'

'Yes, they told me about that in London.'

'There was no sign of a body in the ruins, so it seems more than likely they smuggled him out of the colony and into China. They'd never have gone to the trouble of attacking a British torpedo boat unless there was a very good reason for it.'

Carradine grunted something in reply, then turned his head to glance through the rear window. The headlights of a solitary car showed some distance behind them. Although Kellaway was driving slowly, the other vehicle showed no sign of catching up with them. Sharply, he said: 'That car behind us. It's been there for some minutes now, just keeping pace with us.'

Kellaway glanced in the mirror, his face tight. 'Could be some of the other passengers who were on the plane with you. This is the only road into Kowloon.'

'Maybe. But I've got the feeling whoever is in it may be interested in us, or more precisely in me.'

'You want me to try to lose them?' Kellaway asked.

Carradine smiled to himself at the note

41

of eagerness in the other's tone. Apart from what had happened to Chao Lin, this was perhaps the only bit of excitement which had come along to brighten the other's life out here. He shook his head. 'No. Wait until you come to some convenient spot where you can pull off the road, then put out the headlights and we'll take a closer look at them. Are there any sharp bends in this road?'

The other pursed his lips momentarily, then nodded. 'One up ahead, about a quarter of a mile. There's also a short cul-de-sac leading off it to the right.'

'Good. Then get in there.'

Jerking his head around, he kept an eye on the twin spotlights behind them as Kellaway eased his foot down slightly on the accelerator to widen the distance between them. They drove over the brow of a hill with the lights of Kowloon stretched out before them. Then, almost before Carradine was aware of it, the other spun hard on the wheel and they roared into a narrow, dark entrance, with a tangle of brush at the far end blocking any further movement.

Snapping off the headlights, Kellaway switched off the ignition. Tension built up swiftly in the warm, dark silence. Then there came the muted purr of the car which had been following them. Jerking the Luger from his shoulder holster, Carradine opened the door and stood up, then crouched down behind the car. Kellaway remained seated behind the wheel, his body hunched slightly forward. There was a tense expression on his face, the lips twisted into a faint grimace.

Headlights showed along the road at the mouth of the alley. They grew brighter as the sound of the car increased. It was moving slowly, almost as if the driver suspected what they had done. Then it glided past. He caught a brief glimpse of the man in the driver's seat, leaning forward as though peering intently through the windscreen. There were at least two men in the back, dark anonymous shadows from which no detail emerged.

Two of his fellow passengers, as Kellaway thought? Or was his presence here in Hong Kong known to the enemy? The sound of the car engine faded a little.

With an effort, he forced himself to relax. Then, abruptly, the sound came again, growing louder. The car was coming back! He opened his mouth to yell a warning to Kellaway. Before a single sound could be uttered, the car was there, jerking to a halt opposite the cul-de-sac, the harsh squeal of rubber against the road surface sounding painfully in his ears. Pulling his head down, he jerked up the gun, every nerve in his body screaming that there was danger here. The beam of a powerful flashlight lanced from the rear of the car and touched the boot of Kellaway's car, then slid on, probing the shadows. Someone said something in a high sing-song voice.

Carradine had a momentary glimpse of some dark object which flew through the air towards him, bounced off the wing of the car and hit the hard-packed dirt a few feet from where he crouched. Instinctively he hurled himself forward, shoulder halfway under the protruding bonnet as the night erupted in a cavernous roar of smoke and flame. Ears ringing from the thunderous explosion, his body jarred and shaken by the blast, he held his arms

44

over his head as bits of debris began to fall all about him. There was a tinkle of shattered glass and the licking of red-tongued flame at the edge of his vision.

For a moment he lay half-conscious, struggling to focus all of his senses. Then, choking and coughing, he hoisted himself to his feet. In the distance, above the roaring in his ears, he heard the unmistakable sound of a car engine being revved up, and saw through tear-blurred vision the other car jolting forward as the driver gunned it for all his worth down the hill towards Kowloon.

Their car was a shambles. Flames were beginning to lick around the boot and the rear door had been blown completely off its hinges and lay buckled and twisted some feet away from the wreck. Staggering forward, Carradine hauled desperately at the front door. Kellaway lay slumped back in his seat, his face a pale white blur in the dimness. Any minute now that fire would reach the petrol tank and once that went up there wouldn't be a chance in hell of getting Kellaway out of the blazing wreck.

Savagely, his head swimming, he struggled with the warped door, cursing futilely as the sharp metal tore at his fingers until blood trickled warmly down his wrists. Glass lay over the front seat and over Kellaway's back and shoulders but he did not seem to be badly injured. The blast must have knocked him forward so that he had struck his head on the dashboard. Carradine groaned aloud as he heaved with all of the strength left in his pulverised body. Any second now and even if the naked flames did not reach the highly sensitive fuel, the heat alone would be sufficient to ignite it. If he was to save himself, he would have to get away from the burning car and leave Kellaway to his fate.

With one final desperate heave, he contracted the muscles of his arms and shoulders and dragged back on the door handle with all of his weight. With a high-pitched screech of tortured, rending metal, the door gave, opening so abruptly that he fell back on to the dirt with the mass of metal on top of his bruised chest. Without pausing to think coherently, he sucked a gust of air into his lungs, sprang to his feet, caught Kellaway around the waist and dragged him out of the driver's seat in a single, convulsive movement.

Catching the other beneath the arms, he hauled him madly over the uneven ground, felt the yielding mass of a thorn bush at his back, and kept moving in spite of the inch-long thorns which lacerated his battered flesh even more. Ten yards — fifteen. Then he felt the strength leave his body. Falling forward, he dropped on top of the unconscious man, pulling his head down. Five seconds later, the petrol tank erupted with a belching of flame and smoke. Carradine felt the blast of heat on his face and recoiled instinctively. Sweat boiled out of his body, trickling down into his eyes. Slowly, agonisingly, he pulled Kellaway's inert weight further into the brush. The burning car would make an excellent beacon and he knew it would not be long before someone came out from Kowloon to see what was wrong. He swore softly under his breath. The last thing he wanted right now was publicity of any kind.

Kellaway groaned, stirred weakly, then opened his eyes, staring up at Carradine for a moment uncomprehendingly. Then he put a hand feebly to his head.

'Just lie still for a minute,' Carradine said sharply. 'Once you feel that you can walk, we'd better get the hell out of here. That blaze will be seen for miles.'

'What was it? A bomb?' muttered the other, clenching his teeth as a spasm of pain lanced through him.

'Something like that.' Carradine nodded grimly. 'The enemy is evidently playing for keeps. Though how the hell they knew I was here . . . '

'They have men watching the port and airport.' With an effort, the other pushed himself up onto his hands. 'They have their ways of knowing who comes into Hong Kong.'

'Then the sooner we get out of here, the better.' Bending, he helped Kellaway to his feet. 'This is a damnably bad start. Now that they know I'm here it will make things a hundred times more difficult and dangerous.

'You'll have to lie low once we get to

Victoria,' gasped the other as he forced himself to keep pace with Carradine. The thorn bush was tearing at their arms and legs now with every stumbling step they took, but they were past caring. Their bodies were numbed from shock and pain and behind them they left drops of blood on the black earth.

Half an hour later, they entered the outskirts of Kowloon. Down by the docks, the last ferry to Hong Kong Island lay at the quayside — a smooth, sleek, modern bustle. Already the decks were becoming crowded, mainly with Chinese. They both looked highly conspicuous, but there was nothing else for it but to mingle with the thronging crowd and hope that the enemy, whoever they were, had taken it for granted that the bomb had done its work and their charred, unrecognisable bodies now lay in the smouldering wreckage of the burnt-out car.

The journey across the channel to Victoria was a nightmarish one. Carradine stood by the rail, feeling the cool, salty air touch his stretched body like a balm. He sucked in great gasping lungfuls of air and tried to divorce his mind from his body; to ignore the pain. He was conscious of the packed crowd all around him, hemming him in. He was thankful that, so far, none of the enemy had put in any appearance. In this crowd it would have been utterly impossible to move an inch and he and Kellaway would have been sitting targets. But the journey passed without incident. Scarcely anyone gave them a second glance.

For the time being, he was entirely in Kellaway's hands. He knew nothing of this country. Here, there could be danger every minute, every inch of the way, and he would not recognise it before it was too late. Kellaway, on the other hand, had lived out here long enough to be familiar with the scene and he had readily fallen in with the other's plan to get him into Victoria and under cover for the next two or three days until he found his feet and had been able to formulate a plan to get into China. Whatever happened, it was of the utmost importance that he should make his move as soon as possible; before the tenuous trail which might lead him eventually to Chao Lin grew too cold to follow.

★ ★ ★

Standing under the shower, Carradine hesitated for a moment, gazing down at the dark purple bruises and the long red weals on his naked body. Then he reached out for the valve and turned the water on, gasping as the needle jets struck his body, stinging every muscle and limb. He could just hear Kellaway rummaging around in the other room, pulling open drawers and closing them again.

Carefully he soaped himself down, washing off the grime and congealed blood. When he had finished and was rubbing himself dry with the large, rough towel, he felt a little better. Pain still suffused his body, but the sharp, blistering agony had now subsided to a dull ache and he was able to think more clearly. He recalled a little of the long walk from the quayside to Kellaway's residence, remembering only that he had protested weakly that, once the enemy suspected that he might still be alive, this would be the first place they would think of looking for him. But the other had evidently overruled his objections and now as he slipped into pyjamas, feeling the soft, cool touch of silk against his skin, he was strangely glad that he had given in. He had needed that shower to shock some of the feeling back into him.

'You ready?' Kellaway called.

'Yes.' He came out of the shower. The other poured a stiff drink and handed it to him. 'Better get this down you. You look as though you need it.'

'Thanks.' Carradine tossed the raw whisky down in a single gulp and twisted his lips as the liquor started a fire on its way down into his stomach.

'What now?' asked the other, lowering himself gingerly into a chair. 'If the enemy do know you are here, and why, they won't wait to have another try at you once they realise you're still alive.'

Carradine nodded. 'We've got a busy day ahead of us tomorrow. If possible I'd like to take a look at Chao Lin's office, just in case there is some clue that was missed. Then the sooner I get across to the mainland and over the frontier, the better. My guess is that the trail will stop dead this side of the Chinese border.'

'The chances are a million to one against you picking it up on the other side.'

'I know,' muttered Carradine morosely. 'You don't have to rub in how difficult it's going to be . . . Now, first of all, I shall need papers. Some identity.'

'I think I can get something for you. Anything else? Remember that once you're inside China, you'll be completely on your own. You can trust no one.'

'You don't have to tell me that,' muttered the other grimly. 'I've been in one or two Communist countries in Eastern Europe, but that was child's play compared with this. I'd sooner take my chances inside the Kremlin than in there.' That little affair on the road into Kowloon had told him just how high the dice were stacked against him. God, but the Chinese Intelligence must be far more efficient than they had ever realised back in London. If he did succeed in getting back, he should be able to put the Chief wise on a few points. Up until now, they had considered the Chinese Communists as a rather backward lot where military intelligence was concerned. At that very moment, he had a far different picture of how they operated.

He refilled his glass and sipped his drink more slowly this time, savouring each mouthful. Gradually the whisky made him feel sleepy, a deep lethargy seeping over him in waves so that he could scarcely keep his eyes open.

'You must be all in,' said Kellaway apologetically. He rose to his feet. 'Forgive me. I'm afraid I'm not being much of a host tonight. Too many things have been happening. I'll show you to your room.'

★　★　★

The Headquarters of the Chinese Counter-Intelligence Organisation were housed in a large modern building on the outskirts of Canton, an ugly erection of six stories standing head and shoulders above all of the neighbouring buildings as though certain of its own importance. The two lower floors housed the typists and cypher clerks and the third floor contained the communication centre, while on the fourth, behind locked rooms, was the Records Section. At the far end of the Records Section, a narrow stairway led up to the floor above. Here, behind doors guarded by men armed with submachine-guns, were the conference rooms in which devious operations were planned and set in motion. The top floor, reached by an express lift operating directly from the ground floor, housed the secret headquarters of General Lung Chan, head of the Counter-Intelligence Service.

On that particular morning, there were five men seated in the large room on the topmost floor. In the red plush chair beneath the large portrait of Mao Tse Tung sat General Lung Chan. In spite of the gross hugeness of his body, the yellow khaki tunic hung loosely on him with no hint of neatness. His cap rested on the polished table in front of him, beside the small pile of dossiers, the topmost one of which was open at the front page.

The four other men were the respective heads of the various sections who worked under Lung Chan. They sat forward in their stiff, hard chairs and watched him impassively, waiting for him to give some sign that the conference was to begin.

For a long moment, there was a deep silence in the room, then Lung Chan reached out a carefully manicured hand and placed it palm downward on the open page of the dossier.

'You have all read the reports concerning the traitor, Chao Lin. Since it was found necessary to bring him here to Canton, there has been the expected activity in the British Intelligence Service. One of their agents was flown to Hong Kong two days ago to look into Chao Lin's disappearance.' The voice was flat, lacking emotion. 'My recommendation was that this agent be eliminated before he reached Kowloon. His name and record are in our files and it was not anticipated that there would be any difficulty, particularly since we received the fullest possible information as to his movements from our agent in Hong Kong.

'However.' He paused significantly. 'The attempt was a dismal failure.' The bland features did not change but there was a subtle alteration in the silky voice. 'This is the kind of mistake which cannot be tolerated. Those responsible have already been removed.' The narrowed eyes lifted, resting on the face of the man directly opposite him at the far end of the table. Chin Wang, Section Head of the State Security Division, forced himself to meet the inscrutable gaze without flinching, knowing that the thinly veiled threat was directed at him and his group.

'They were two of my most trusted men,' he said defensively. 'It was pure chance that this British agent escaped. He must have been warned.'

'It is not a question of whether or not he was warned. Every enemy agent knows that there will be danger when he is assigned to a mission. It should have been obvious that he would be prepared for an attempt on his life.'

There was no answer to that from the men around the table. Each of them was glad he was not in Chin Wang's shoes. There were bound to be certain repercussions because of this unfortunate failure. Men who made mistakes suddenly discovered that they were expendable as far as the state was concerned.

'It is indeed fortunate that we can get information on every move that he makes. His name is — ' Lung Chan consulted the dossier before him, although there was no necessity for him to do so since he knew almost everything about the enemy. ' — Carradine. Age twenty-nine. Has been a member of the British Secret Service for almost five years, the last three of them in their specialist espionage branch serving overseas. You will all find his photograph in the folder in front of you. Expert in karate and judo, a crack shot with the Luger, the gun which he seems to prefer. Has a high pain threshold and we can also assume that he knows nothing of the secrets of the British organisation. He will have been given merely the bare facts of this case and it will then be up to him to act accordingly.'

'Then torture will get nothing from him?' inquired the head of Records.

Lung Chan bowed his head slightly in the acquiescence. 'That is so. We are not interested in anything he may be able to tell us concerning the enemy's organisation. The directive we have received is that he must be killed. Our latest information is that he intends to enter China to follow the trail of Chao Lin. He will almost certainly attempt to cross the border somewhere here.' The massive bulk heaved itself from the chair and crossed the room to where a large map hung on the wall. Lung Chan prodded it with a stubby finger. 'The order is that he must be allowed to enter China. He must not be killed until he is on Chinese territory. I want that perfectly understood by every department. The time — and the method — will be chosen by a higher authority.'

A faint, half-heard sigh eddied through the room. For a moment, the eyes of the men seated around the table brightened perceptibly.

Lung Chan paused, then turned from his deliberation of the map. 'This mission has the approval of our beloved Mao Tse Tung himself. From this, you will all realise that failure cannot be contemplated, or tolerated. The world has thought little of our intelligence services. They consider that we are a backward race when it comes to international espionage. Very soon, they will see how wrong they have been. We have all been waiting for this moment. Our scientists have given us some of the most powerful weapons of destruction ever dreamed up by mankind. Once they have been perfected, we can begin the revolution which will eventually end in world conquest for Chinese communism.'

⋆   ⋆   ⋆

Carradine stirred, groaned, then forced himself up from the depths of sleep. Painfully, he eased his long body more comfortably in the bed, the feel of the cool sheets soft on his bruised limbs. It would have been so easy to simply lie there for another hour or more and drift back into the deep sleep in which there was no nagging pain, no rush of thoughts through his mind. But there was work to be done and the thin cries of the street vendors outside his window and the dull roar of traffic told him that Hong Kong was wide awake even at this early hour of the morning. Lazily, he lifted his hand and peered closely at the watch on his wrist. It was still only six-thirty.

Padding across the floor, he pulled on his clothes, flinching a little as the rough cloth touched his lacerated flesh. Going over to the window, he looked out. The broad sweep of the bay was a deep blue in the early morning light, crowded with junks and sampans, with larger vessels tied up at the quay. One of the largest and most important harbours in this part of Asia, it had first come to significance during the Opium Wars more than a century before; it had been chosen as a base for British warships by a young naval officer who had been dismissed for having dared to suggest such a place. Looking at it now, it was difficult to believe that only a little time before, Hong Kong had been only a small settlement. Now they were building on a tremendous scale, great concrete blocks rising to the heavens. Almost all of the capital had been built up by the Chinese here. They were perhaps the best businessmen in the world, knocking down five-storey buildings before they had even been completed, because a ten-storey block of offices would bring in far more profit, then perhaps going on to add a further ten storeys before the building was finally completed. For fifteen minutes, he stood taking in all of the scene which lay stretched out below him, looking out over the barrier of blue water which lay between Hong Kong and the vast mainland of Communist China.

He washed and shaved methodically, then made his way downstairs. Kellaway put in an appearance a few minutes later, still unshaven. 'I'll arrange for breakfast as soon as the servant gets here.'

'How long have you had the servant?'

'Who, Amra Min? About a year. Why?'

'Just naturally suspicious, I guess.' Carradine moved to the window and glanced out into the street. The whole city seemed to have come alive in spite of the early hour.

'You think she may have been the one to give away information?' asked the other unemotionally.

'It's possible. Unless there was anyone

close to Chao Lin who knew of his movements. Somehow I don't think that's possible. If he kept them from you as much as he could, I doubt if he would trust anyone else.'

'I see.' Kellaway shrugged. 'I hadn't thought of that. She may be working with the Red Dragon.'

Carradine raised his brows in mute interrogation.

The other grinned faintly. There was a trace of amusement in his voice as he said: 'That's the name the Chinese Secret Service goes by in this part of the world. It's derived in some way from Mao Tse Tung. They believe that he is the Red Dragon who will liberate China from all of the old ways and make her the greatest military and cultural power on earth.'

'It's certainly a nice thought,' Carradine said dryly. He narrowed his eyes as he caught a glimpse of a slight figure on the opposite side of the street. The girl stood in the shadows made by the grey morning light. She was too far away for him to be able to see her face clearly, but she seemed to be taking a more than normal interest in the house. 'Come over here,' he said sharply. Carefully, he pulled the curtain to one side. 'That girl over there in the shadows. Do you know her at all?'

The other peered out, studied the girl for a moment, then shook his head positively. 'I've never seen her before,' he stated.

'She seems to be watching the house.'

'I doubt it.' The other dismissed the idea as though it was not worth considering seriously. 'Probably waiting for someone.' He walked back into the room.

Carradine remained at the window, keeping an eye on the girl. There was something about her pose which struck a responsive chord in his mind: an attitude of patient waiting, as though she was there to watch for something and was quite prepared to remain in that one position all day if necessary. The tight feeling of uneasiness increased in his mind and there was a tiny warning bell ringing in his brain. It looked as if the enemy were already beginning to close the net a little tighter after their abortive attempt on his life the previous night.

Over breakfast, they discussed his plan for getting across the frontier and into China. As they talked, Carradine realised that Kellaway had not wasted the time he had spent in Hong Kong. He was a mine of information about the place and suggested the best spots where it might be possible to cross the frontier without being seen. Gradually, it emerged that it was not going to be as easy as he had thought. Although tensions had been relaxed appreciably during the past year or so, border checks were stringent and the frontier was well patrolled. The chances of slipping across anywhere in the vicinity of Kowloon were virtually nil. The other possibility which held any hope of success was by sea.

After the Chinese servant had cleared away the breakfast things, Kellaway said softly: 'I think I can manage to find someone who will land you on the Chinese mainland some miles north of Kowloon. There will be the usual enemy patrols, of course, and the risk is still pretty high that you will be spotted before you manage to get ashore.'

'That's a chance I'm prepared to take.'

'Very well. That's settled.' Pushing back his chair, the other rose to his feet. 'We will have to wait until after dark. In the meantime, you want to see what is left of Chao Lin's offices. I'll take you there myself.'

'No.' Carradine shook his head. 'That would be far too conspicuous. I'll go alone if you'll give me the necessary directions.'

'Do you think that would be wise? After all, you're not familiar with the city and — '

Carradine shook his head. 'I'm not an old woman. This is my kind of business. All I want you to do is get me a set of clothes that will make me inconspicuous.' He glanced into the mirror on the wall. 'And the sooner we get around to changing this face of mine, the better. My guess is that they have a picture of me by now and there may be a hundred men looking for me in Hong Kong.'

'There is a man I know who would be willing to do that,' Kellaway said slowly.

'He worked for us on one or two occasions in the past — always for money, but I think he can be trusted.'

'Good. Then get in touch with him and arrange it for this afternoon.' Carradine felt a little easier in his mind now that decisions had been made and things were about to be set in motion. He disliked physical or mental inactivity and was irked by having to sit and twiddle his thumbs while events were passing him by. There was the sensation of inexorable time urging him to a climax; the knowledge that time itself was perhaps the one commodity which was running at a high premium as far as he was concerned. He admitted to himself that, in spite of the dangers and difficulties which undoubtedly lay ahead, he was looking forward to this mission; to being in the middle of trouble and intrigue once again. Those soft days spent in the south of France now lay behind him, already half-forgotten. Before him lay the kind of work for which he had been chosen and trained: mystery and an utterly ruthless enemy who would stop at nothing.

Once the nondescript clothing had been procured for him, he went up into his room and changed into it, then paused in front of the full-length mirror, satisfied with the transformation. Once that make-up expert got to work in the afternoon, it was possible that at a cursory glance he might pass for a Chinese. But would it be a sufficiently expert job to fool the enemy?

3

The Harbingers of Death

The sweet, sickly smell of smoke still hung over the burnt-out shell of the office block as Carradine climbed the stairs. The blackened walls were dotted with shreds of paper and blistered paint and as he reached the top and stood before the door with its splintered glass, the floor creaked ominously beneath his weight. Gaping holes in the roof revealed the sky and here and there, among the fallen, charred beams, were pieces of metal which he recognised as filing cabinets. Going forward gingerly, testing the way with each step, he wrenched open one of the steel drawers. There was nothing inside. Evidently the kidnappers had also taken the opportunity to burn all of the records which had been kept here at the Hong Kong station.

Brushing aside two of the fallen beams,

he entered the inner room behind the concealed entrance, now merely a gaping hole in one wall. The powerful transmitter was a shambles. Every valve had been slashed by some heavy instrument, and the main cable was wrenched from the wall socket. Burnt ash in the middle of the room testified to where confidential and secret papers had been burned in the fire.

Sooner or later — possibly sooner — London would have to start up another station here. This part of Asia was a hotbed of intrigue and tension and it was absolutely essential that they should have their eyes and ears here, watchful for any sign that the Communists were preparing to foment more trouble. In the meantime, he had his own job to do. A quick, all-embracing glance around the empty shell was sufficient to tell him he would learn nothing of value here; the enemy had been far too thorough in their work of destruction.

Picking his way through the debris, he made his way back to the door. He was less than three feet from it when he heard

70

the faint sound. At first, his mind did not register the direction from which it came. There had been no one in the room, he was sure of that — so there could be only one direction from which danger would come. He threw his head back and glanced up at the gaping hole where the roof had once been. The head and shoulders of a man were just visible near the edge of the hole. He caught a fragmentary glimpse of a snarling face, lips thinned back over yellow teeth. Then a heavy piece of masonry toppled forward as the other heaved it savagely. Scarcely pausing to think, Carradine acted instinctively, his legs moving almost of their own volition, hurling him forward. Arms ahead of him, he crashed through the splintered doorway. Something scraped the back of his heel and there was a shuddering crash behind him as the hundredweight of stone and concrete smashed into the floor. Giving a final thrust with his legs, he dropped flat onto his face, sucking air down into his heaving lungs.

Seconds later, a dark figure rose from behind one of the charred desks and came towards him. The sunlight streaming down through the hole in the roof glinted blue off the blade of the knife in the other's hand.

Half-lying on the floor, Carradine tensed. There was no time to go for the heavy Luger in its holster. By the time his fingers closed around the butt, there would be a knife blade between his ribs. He caught the glitter of vicious eagerness on the Oriental face; the snarling grin. Getting his left leg under him, he waited, not once moving his gaze from the other's eyes. When a man was moving in for the kill, especially one who firmly believed he held all of the cards, it was his eyes that would give away the moment when he intended to make his move.

For some reason, the other seemed strangely hesitant about coming in now. He hung back, the knife still gripped in his hand, the blade pointed directly at Carradine. Now what the hell — ?

A brief moment later something whistled past his head and stuck quivering in the wooden floor a couple of inches from his left hand. The knife had been aimed at him from above. He had completely forgotten about the man on the roof. Before he could turn to meet this new danger, the other had dropped lightly into the room. A hand caught Carradine around the mouth and jammed hard into the small of his back, and he could smell the dirt and grime on the other's body as the man began to haul back on his head so that his unprotected chest was presented to the Chinaman in front of him. The other drew back his hand with the knife balanced delicately between finger and thumb.

Drawing a gasp of air through his tightly clenched teeth, feeling his senses reel beneath that stranglehold on his throat, Carradine exerted all of his strength, his legs jerking upward as he pulled hard on his attacker. With a wild, thin cry the man flew over his shoulders at the same moment that the other killer hurled the knife. Retaining his grip, Carradine held the killer in front of him, going down on one knee at the same time.

He felt the man shudder convulsively as the knife thudded home into his attacker's back, and knew from the sudden limpness that it had struck home to the heart. The fingers loosened around his throat. Desperately, he drew in a deep breath and forced his head to clear. There was no time to think of his own aches and bruises if he was to stay alive.

Pushing the dead man away from him, he heaved himself to his feet and moved in on the other man. Stronger fingers with long but splintered nails flicked out for his eyes, seeking to gouge and blind. Carradine side-stepped and used a savage karate chop against the other's neck, but the man was already rolling sideways and the blow did not have the effect he had intended. Dirty nails scratched a bloody line down his cheek. A knee caught him in the groin. Biting down on the yell of pain, he gritted his teeth, took a firm grip on the man's arm and whirled him off his feet. With a shrill scream, the other stumbled sideways and fell with a crash against a wall.

Almost as if his body had been made of rubber, the other bounced back, his head lowered. The top of his skull caught Carradine squarely in the pit of the stomach, knocking him backward off his feet. The edge of one of the desks hit him between the shoulder blades, knocking all of the air out of his lungs. Carradine's only reaction was to drop to his knees as the other dropped on top of him, hoping to pin him down with his weight. The body of the second killer lay only a few inches away and it was evidently his enemy's intention to lean over and pull the knife from the man's back in order to use it on Carradine.

A red mist hovered in front of his vision as he attempted to defend himself. He felt a foot hammer into his stomach, then the other had an iron grip on his throat and was squeezing inexorably with all of his strength, his eyes glinting with a killing fever. For a second, panic threatened to take hold of Carradine's mind and was on the point of directing his actions. Then, swiftly, his mind orientated itself and he felt as cold as ice inside. Panic was no good at a time like this. He had to act coolly and calmly and allow his rigid training to take over. He allowed the other to retain his grip on his throat, concentrating instead on tensing the muscles of his thighs and legs as he got them beneath the man's body. His eyes were bulging and it seemed that the throbbing, hammering pressure inside his head must surely burst it asunder before very long.

Desperately, he heaved upward with all of his remaining strength. For a moment, he thought sickeningly that it would not be enough. Then the claw-like hold on his throat was gone. He had a vague impression of the other hurtling backward, taken completely by surprise, caught off-balance. For a moment the Chinaman was poised in front of the smoke-blackened window which overlooked the street more than twenty feet below, his arms flailing futilely as he struggled ineffectually to keep his balance. Then, with a wild, high-pitched scream, he was gone.

Dazedly, Carradine pushed himself to his knees and stayed there for a long moment as he fought to rid his mind of the blackness of unconsciousness. Slowly he got to his feet and stood swaying for a few seconds, then staggered towards the window, feeling the cool air flow against his face. Glancing down, he saw the sprawled figure on the pavement below, arms and legs outflung. A small crowd had already begun to gather.

It was time to leave; even here in Hong Kong where life was cheap, there could be awkward questions to answer. Already he seemed to have attracted far too much unwelcome publicity. How the enemy knew of his whereabouts and his actions, he was not sure. As he made his way down towards the offices on the lower floors where the fire had not reached, he recalled the girl he had seen standing in the shadows opposite Kellaway's house that morning. Was she the informer? It was just possible that, in spite of all the precautions he had taken against being followed, she had somehow managed to trail him here and had warned two of her confederates, resulting in this attempt on his life.

There were several people in the corridors as he made his way quickly towards the rear of the building. A few glanced curiously at him but no one made a move to stop him. As he reached the rear exit, there came the thin wheep of a whistle from the street at the front. The police had arrived on the scene of violence. There was a narrow alley at the back of the office block and he walked swiftly along it, thankful to see that it was deserted. From close by came various sounds and echoes. He could hear the roar of the traffic which never seemed to stop.

At the end of the alley he found himself in a broader street lined with shops and a wide variety of traders. It was packed with a jostling sea of humanity. Shrill voices argued and bargained for food at the rickety stalls. Here and there were old men seated drinking tea, their faces staring vacantly at the stream of life which milled around them.

On an instinct, he felt the weapon in his belt. The metal was cold and hard and reassuring against his shirt. He shouldered his way through the crowd. Here, at least, he felt temporarily safe. In this seething mass of humanity, it was doubtful if he could be followed. There seemed scarcely any room in which to move. At first sight, it was as if the whole of Hong Kong's Chinese population had decided to come to the market that morning and were agglomerated here in this short stretch of road. The shrill cries of the hawkers lifted on all sides. Here and there, he noticed the fortune-tellers seated in front of their curtained recesses, broadcasting their abilities to all and sundry. There was also a sprinkling of Europeans and he deliberately gave them a wide berth in case he was recognised as one of them and someone tried to draw him into conversation.

He had almost reached the end of the line of stalls when his eyes caught a glimpse of someone standing in the doorway of one of the tall buildings. His breath rasped sharply between his teeth. He could not be absolutely certain, but he felt almost sure that it was the girl he had noticed a few hours before. There was something disturbingly familiar about the attitude of watchful waiting and even as he halted in his tracks, he saw that she was eyeing him with more than normal curiosity.

Very well, he thought grimly, it was

time he had a showdown with her, whoever she was, even if it ended up with him
having made a mistake about her identity
and a fool of himself.

A knot of milling women interposed
themselves between him and the doorway
and he thrust his way half-angrily through
them, muttering apologies under his breath.
For a brief moment, he lost sight of the
girl. When he lifted his head once more,
the doorway was empty. Grunting an oath,
he walked swiftly to the end of the street.
There was no sign of her whatever.

He began walking slowly along the
street, almost empty in comparison to
that which he had just left, his eyes roving
along either side, alert for trouble. He no
longer needed any further warning that
since arriving here he had been a marked
man. Too many people knew who he was
and were interested in his demise. Twenty
yards further on, he came to a narrow
side street which opened out to his left.
Perhaps the girl had gone down there,
he decided. A quick glance about him
revealed that no one appeared to be
watching him. The stink in the alley was

overpowering. He wrinkled his nostrils, then forced his attention to the ramshackle buildings which sprouted on either side. Most of them had been abandoned and were boarded up — and yet in spite of this outward appearance, he gained the impression that, at times, they were quite fully occupied. There were so many Chinese in Hong Kong that no house which offered even the most menial shelter was left empty for long.

The scent of danger was all about him. He had the unmistakable impression that his feet were leading him into a trap and he fingered the butt of the pistol instinctively.

A sudden sound broke in on his thoughts. It came from behind him. Whirling swiftly, his body balanced on his toes, he saw the big truck which had nosed its way into the alley. The bumpers scraped the walls on either side. The engine was suddenly revved up as the vehicle lurched forward, wheels spinning in the dust, throwing white clouds up on either side.

He could just see the face of the man crouched over the wheel as the truck came straight for him. There was no doubting the other's intention. Turning, he began to run as the vehicle came after him, gaining with every second. So the enemy had not lost his trail. They had simply been biding their time, waiting until he was clear of the milling crowd, where they could take care of him with little or no trouble.

The end of the alley lay two hundred yards ahead of him, blocked by a high wall. One glimpse of its smooth surface, and the fact that it was at least twelve feet in height, told him it would be out of the question to try to scale it. Even if he succeeded in getting a grip on the top by jumping for it, the front of that truck would ram him into it before he was able to clamber over it to safety, crushing him to death against the solid concrete. Wildly, he peered at the buildings on either side as he ran, his breath harsh in his throat, burning in his chest. The roar of the powerful engine was like a growing thunder in his ears.

Tugging the Luger from his belt, he threw a quick look over his shoulder, steadied himself and loosed off a couple of snap shots. The first shattered the windscreen into a thousand glittering fragments, but went wide of the driver. The second broke the offside headlight. Still the truck came on relentlessly. There was not even the slightest check in its speed.

Carradine continued to run, knowing, however, that his unspeakable end would come inevitably. There was no way for him to escape. He stumbled, picked himself up, and ran towards one side of the street, wondering vaguely if he might be able to squeeze himself against the wall. There was a narrow doorway just ahead of him, but the closed door seemed too solid for him to be able to break it in.

God, why had he been so insane as to come down here when it had been so damnably obvious that it might be a trap? Why hadn't he gone back to Kellaway's place right away? He set his teeth in a vicious grin and drew level with the door. *All right, damn you,* he thought savagely, *get it over and done with!*

The truck, bouncing and swaying a little, was less than twenty feet away. He turned and lifted the gun, knowing that even if he did succeed in killing the driver with his next shot, nothing on God's earth would stop that juggernaut now.

Then, almost before he was aware that anything had happened, the door opened abruptly; an arm came out, grabbed him by the wrist and almost yanked him off his feet as he was pulled through the door. He heard it slam shut behind him and blinked his eyes against the dimness. Abruptly he stiffened, and felt his heart skip a beat as a girl's voice said softly: 'Those men seem determined to kill you, don't they?'

Carradine had been in the act of thrusting the heavy Luger back into its holster. Now he tightened his grip on the weapon. He was looking into the face of the girl he had noticed in the market — the same girl, he felt sure, he had seen earlier that morning outside Kellaway's residence.

'All right,' he said shortly. 'There are some questions I want to ask you. I've been — '

'Later,' she said urgently, cutting him

short. 'First we must get away from here.' She pulled him away from the door. 'Those men out there aren't going to wait long before they surround this house and come in for us. Follow me. Quickly!'

In spite of his suspicions about her, Carradine recognised the logic of what she said. The squeal of brakes outside told him that the truck had come to a halt. He fancied he heard the sound of raised voices in the alley. Keeping the gun in his right hand, he allowed the girl to lead him through the empty rooms of the house. There was a flight of stairs at the end of one of the rooms and without pausing, the girl ran lightly up them, motioning him to follow. When he hesitated for a second, she hissed: 'We can't go out of the back door. It's boarded up tight and they'll be expecting us to do that. We must do this my way.'

'All right. But the first wrong move you make and I won't hesitate to hit you over the head with this.' He nodded menacingly at the gun in his hand. For a second she smiled as though secretly amused, then nodded.

Less than three minutes later, they came out on the top floor. Carradine looked about him. Without saying a word, the girl went over to the grimy window, opened it and looked out, then motioned him forward. 'This is the only way out without them seeing us,' she said softly. She looked at him appraisingly. 'It isn't going to be easy.'

Carradine looked over her shoulder. There was a narrow balcony just beyond the window, jutting out over the alley below, but no way down that he could see.

'I presume we're not going to jump,' he said, a faint note of sarcasm in his tone.

'We shall make our way across to the building opposite.' She pointed.

Looking up, he noticed the steel bar which stretched across the alley to the roof of the opposite house.

In answer to the unspoken question on his face, she said: 'We must swing ourselves over. It's the only chance. Do you think you can do it?'

For a second he stared down at her upturned face in amazement. 'Over that?'

He thrust the gun into his belt. 'I think I could probably manage it, but you — '

'Don't worry on my account,' she murmured. 'I'm used to heights. I work with an acrobatic troupe. Just do as I do and you'll be all right.'

Carradine tried to keep the surprise from his face as she climbed easily onto the narrow balcony, paused for a moment, then jumped for the pole, hooked her fingers around it and began to swing herself, hand over hand, across the alley, thirty feet or so below. There was no doubt, he was forced to admit to himself, that she was as good as she had claimed.

Reaching up, he grasped the pole and swung himself out into space. The ground below him seemed a very long way away and he forced himself not to look down, but to concentrate on swinging himself over. Before he was three-quarters of the way across, the strain on his arms was like fire in his shoulders and wrist muscles. The girl had crossed with an effortless ease which made it apparent that she was quite used to this sort of thing. Determined not to be shown up by a mere girl, he gritted his teeth and kept on going.

After what seemed an eternity, he reached the end of the pole, swung his legs over the top of the balcony and released his hold. His heart was pumping in his chest.

'You're out of training,' said the girl, laughing.

Carradine felt himself flushing. 'Perhaps.' He forced the grin in return. 'But at least we're here. What now?'

'Those fools will search the other place for us, but by the time they realise we have slipped through their fingers, we will be a long way from here and they will never find us.'

Carradine waited until they were on the ground floor before catching the girl's arm, halting her roughly. 'Before we go any further,' he said grimly, 'there are some questions I want answered. Just who are you? How do I know I can trust you?'

'If I had been working for the Red Dragon, would I have got you out of there?' she said contemptuously. 'I would simply have left you in that alley where they would have crushed you to a pulp.'

'Then why are you doing this?'

'Perhaps I should introduce myself. My name is Ts'ai Luan. Chao Lin is my uncle.'

'I think I understand.'

'Do you? I wonder.' A pause, then she went on hurriedly: 'I was working in Canton when I heard that he had been kidnapped. I came here as quickly as I could to try to discover what had happened and where they had taken him. I knew that it was the work of the Red Dragon.'

'Just a minute.' Carradine's tone was shocked. 'You say that you were in Canton? Then how on earth — '

'Did I get to Hong Kong?' She smiled. For a moment there was an answering sparkle in the dark eyes beneath the long black lashes. For the first time, he saw how beautiful she really was. Before, her face had been merely a half-glimpsed thing seen in the shadows.

She went on: 'That was easy. There are ways of getting in and out of China if you know them.'

'And how did you find out about me?'

'That was not so easy. I knew the sort of work my uncle did for British Intelligence. He told me little, of course. But he always used to say that there might come a time when the Communists would become suspicious of him; would discover what he was doing, and then they would try to kill him. He said that if anything did happen to him, the British would send another agent here to try to find out what had happened, maybe to take his place.'

Carradine nodded slowly. This was an added complication he had not allowed for. Yet in a way he was grateful for it. Without the girl's help, he would almost certainly not be alive now.

'I knew that when anyone did arrive from London, they would meet with Mr. Kellaway, so I decided to keep a close watch on his house for any visitors.'

'Then it was you I noticed this morning.'

She nodded slowly. 'The Red Dragon have many spies everywhere. I had to be very careful. It was why I followed you to my uncle's offices. I guessed that they might try to kill you.'

Carradine was forced to admit that her story was plausible. Yet could he believe it, even now? The enemy was devilishly clever. It was just possible they had decided to have a second string to their bow in the shape of this beautiful girl.

'You make it all seem very logical,' he said at length. 'There is only one thing I don't understand. Someone in Hong Kong is feeding information back to the Red Dragon. It's obvious that they know most of my moves beforehand.'

The girl's eyes narrowed slightly. 'There is something my uncle told me which may explain this. It concerns Mr. Kellaway.'

'The man who worked with your uncle?'

'He was suspicious of Kellaway. He had the feeling that he could not be trusted. That is why he did not take him into his confidence as he might normally have done. Perhaps he is the man who is giving this information to the Red Dragon.'

'That seems hardly likely.' Carradine did not add that the Chief, back in

London, trusted Kellaway implicitly.

Ts'ai Luan shrugged her shoulders disdainfully. 'All I know is what my uncle told me.' She eyed him shrewdly. 'What are your plans now? I can take you somewhere where you will be safe until you want to get into China. I can also get you there without any trouble. I have friends in Canton. The other members of the troupe are all against the Communist regime there, but it is dangerous to even whisper against Mao Tse Tung while inside China. The Red Dragon have ears and eyes everywhere. No one can be trusted.' She looked at him calmly.

Carradine could see no guile in her face but that did not dispel the uneasiness in his mind. True, she had just saved his life at the risk of her own, but that was not conclusive proof of her genuine desire to help him further.

'Now listen.' He put nonchalance into his voice and placed one hand under her chin, tilting her head up. 'I have a job to do. You seem to know far more about me than I do about you. In fact I know nothing at all about you. For all I know, you too could be a Red Dragon agent sent here to lure me into China where a dozen of your fellow countrymen would be waiting to pop up and finish me. We've got to stop fooling ourselves and be quite serious. You've made an accusation against Kellaway. Yet you have no proof to back it up.'

'That is perfectly true. You must, of course, make up your own mind which course you are going to take. Clearly nothing I can do or say is going to change your mind about Kellaway. I can't even prove that Chao Lin is my uncle. Yet all I know is that, whatever you do, I intend to find him, wherever they have taken him. When I find him, I shall kill those responsible.' There was a note of fierce determination in her voice which told Carradine that she was quite capable of doing exactly as she threatened. The sharp tingle of suspicion faded just a little. In spite of himself, he suddenly found that he wanted to believe her.

'I intend to enter China tonight by — ' He remembered security and went on quickly. 'No matter how I get there. If you do go through with your crazy plan of trying to find Chao Lin yourself, perhaps we may meet again, somewhere.'

She caught at his arm, her fingers digging into his flesh with a steely strength. 'Just one thing. Whatever you do, don't trust Kellaway too far. Whether you believe me or not it doesn't matter. Just be very careful. And if you do change your mind, go down to the quayside at nine o'clock tonight. I have a small boat waiting there. It has a yellow dragon on the sail, the only one of its kind. I'll wait until half-past nine. If you come, we'll go together. If not, then I shall go without you.'

'I'll remember that.' He gently disengaged his arm. 'Now I'd better get back to Kellaway or he'll think something has happened.'

It was not until he was approaching the other's house on the side of Victoria Peak that the irony of that statement struck him.

★   ★   ★

Seated in front of the mirror, Carradine stared intently back at the face which peered out at him from the crystal glass. It was not the face he had known for more years than he cared to remember. He felt certain that none of his friends back in London would ever recognise the slant-eyed Oriental features as those of Steve Carradine.

The face surgeon had certainly known his job. Carradine only hoped that it would pass muster once he was inside Communist China. His whole life would depend on it. He checked the watch which he had taken from his wrist. It was a quarter to nine. Apart from the general background noise of the city, it was quiet. Kellaway had left half an hour earlier to check the preparations he had made for the boat to take him over to the Chinese mainland.

In spite of the troubles in his mind, Carradine felt his thoughts turning more and more to the fascinating girl he had encountered that morning. Just how much truth was there in her story? Could Kellaway possibly be a double agent? One part of the girl's story seemed to ring true. If she was a Chinese Red Dragon agent, then why had she gone to so much trouble to save his life when those killers in the truck had him at their mercy?

He reached a sudden decision. There was one way of checking on Ts'ai Luan's story. If Kellaway was working with the enemy, then he had to have some means of getting in touch with them. Even after he himself had arrived in Hong Kong, someone had been passing information about him to the Chinese. Sending word by means of a messenger was far too risky. Kellaway would never have dared to use a go-between. It would have been much too conspicuous. That meant only one thing. There had to be a radio transmitter somewhere in the house if what the girl had said was true.

In the next ten minutes he made a quick but thorough survey of the rooms, but discovered nothing out of the ordinary. He had not expected a transmitter to be somewhere where it could be easily found and this failure did not deter him. The cellars too were empty, apart from several large packing cases which were also devoid of any contents. Thoughtfully, he made his way up to the topmost floor and glanced towards a skylight which appeared to have been recently built into the ceiling of the corridor between two of the bed-rooms. Placing a chair beneath it, he managed to slide aside the glass cover. Hooking his fingers tightly around the edge of the open-ing, he hauled himself up, swinging his legs until they locked inside the opening, then finally straightening up, hanging on to one side of the thick wooden cross-beams to steady himself. Here too there were several large cases, one in particular, over in the far corner, much larger than the rest, and oblong in shape.

Ignoring the others, he ripped off the lid. The wooden cover protected the gleaming grey metal of the modern transmitter which reposed inside. For a moment he gazed at it thoughtfully, then picked up the small black notebook which lay beside the apparatus. The first page contained a series of names and addresses and Carradine's eyes narrowed as he saw that some of them were of places in Canton. Several of the other pages were covered with a series of English letters and Chinese characters.

Well, this appeared pretty definite. He sat back on his heels, turning over this fresh piece of evidence in his mind. One thing was certain: if he carried out the plan he had formulated with Kellaway, there would surely be a welcoming party waiting for him once he set foot on Chinese soil. He could visualise what his fate would be once he fell into their hands. So what to do now?

Replacing the book inside the case, he put the lid back on the box and lowered himself through the square opening, sliding the glass back into place after dropping lightly onto the chair. In spite of this disturbing discovery, he experienced a sudden sense of relief. At the back of his mind he knew he had been wanting the girl to be proved right, even if it meant finding out that Kellaway was working with the enemy. Again, he made an impulsive decision. If Kellaway had been passing information about his movements to the enemy on the mainland, then he could no longer go ahead with the original plan.

He had to get out of there before

Kellaway returned; had to get to the quayside and meet the girl. He checked the wristwatch which lay on the table — to have taken it with him would have been a direct giveaway — and saw that it was now five minutes past nine. Outside, it was already dark. If he hurried he might just be able to get there before she left.

Pausing only to strap on the holster and the heavy Luger, and pick up the papers with which Kellaway had so thoughtfully provided him, he let himself out of the rear door.

The moon shone whitely on the streets as he made his way quickly in the direction of the harbour.

He stopped at the bottom of a narrow alley and looked quickly about him with an all-encompassing glance. The road to his left leading down towards the quayside less than half a mile away, with the waters of the narrow channel gleaming palely in the moonlight and starshine, was deserted. He was on the point of moving out into it when he caught sight of three dark figures moving in his direction. Swiftly, he pressed himself into the shadow of a doorway and held his breath until it hurt in his lungs as the men drew level with him. They were talking earnestly in low voices, speaking in Chinese. Carradine stiffened. Two of the men he did not recognise — the usual type of Chinese coolie one met in Hong Kong, with narrow faces and bright eyes that gleamed ferally in the dimness.

It was easy to believe that they could be hatchet men for the Red Dragon operating inside Hong Kong. But he did not give them a second thought as they moved past his hiding place without even suspecting his presence there; for it was the third man who caught and held his attention. Evidently Chao Lin had known what he was about when he had suspected his Number Two of working in collaboration with the enemy. *The third man was Kellaway!*

The trio continued up the street for a little way, then paused beneath one of the lights. Kellaway had a piece of paper in his hand and was holding it so that the other two could see clearly. They were too far away for Carradine to pick out any of their conversation, even if he had been able to understand the language fluently. But it was not so difficult to guess at the gist of it. These, he felt certain, were the men who would have been waiting on board the boat to ferry him across to the spot on the Chinese mainland; the men he would have accompanied unsuspectingly, going trustingly to his death.

He waited for what seemed an eternity, but which could only have been three minutes at most. Then the men moved away into the stretch of anonymous darkness which lay beyond the solitary lamp. The sound of their footsteps died away into the echoing distance. Stepping out of the doorway, he made his way rapidly to the harbour, scanning the multitude of junks for the one bearing the yellow dragon on its square-cut sail.

4

Night Landing

'So you now believe that I was telling you the truth this morning?' Ts'ai Luan pulled strongly on the rope, tightened it, then motioned to Carradine to draw up the anchor. 'What made you change your mind?'

'I found his secret transmitter less than an hour ago,' Carradine said simply. 'I also passed him on the way back to his house with two hatchet men. No doubt they have been planning the best method of getting rid of me before I could start more trouble.'

The girl seemed to sense the bitterness in his thoughts. 'I have seen too much of this double-dealing inside China,' she murmured philosophically as the junk began to move slowly out of the harbour. 'I have been forced to kill sometimes.'

'You?' Surprise tinged Carradine's

voice. He stared at her face, in profile against the pale darkness of the sky as she sat in the stern. It was a calm, beautiful face — one he would never have associated with violence and death. Then he recalled all that the people of China had been forced to endure since Japan had attacked them thirty years before. Then it had been the all-conquering soldiers of Nippon, and afterwards the bitter civil conflict between the Communists and the Nationalists under Chiang Kai-shek.

'The battle for freedom in China is far from won,' she said simply. 'Because under the Communist one either obeys blindly, or dies. It is as simple as that. Nobody is now allowed to think for themselves.'

'But surely you can't hope to win. Your efforts must be mere pinpricks against the regime.'

'Perhaps. But so long as the spirit of freedom is kept alive, they cannot afford to relax and someday there may be a new revolution.'

'At the moment, my job is to try to prevent a world revolution. So far, Russia seems to have accepted the fact of peaceful co-existence. But whether the present leaders of your country will is another problem. Personally, I doubt it. It seems to me that once they firmly believe they have a superior weapon to any possessed by the West — or by Russia — they will start on that plan for world conquest. If they do, then it will very likely be the bloodiest revolution this world has ever known.'

By now, they were well out from Hong Kong Harbour, out on the gentle swell of the sea with a faint breeze blowing from the south-east and only the bright stars and the pale moon giving them any light. It was just possible, in their glimmering starshine, to make out the rising mountains ahead of them, marking their destination. The girl guided the boat with an uncanny instinct. It was possible, Carradine thought idly, that she was navigating by the stars, but somehow he doubted it. The soft swell almost sent him to sleep as he sat near the big sail, listening to the faint to slap of the water against the hull.

Out here in the midst of all the quiet

stillness, the danger and violence which he knew were to come seemed so far away as to have faded into utter insignificance. Only the hard feel of the Luger automatic in his belt gave any indication of it.

It must have been two hours later that the girl came forward and laid a hand on his arm. In a low voice she whispered: 'We must be very quiet and careful now. The Communists have men patrolling the coast. They look mostly for smugglers or people trying to get out of the country and across to Hong Kong but they also know that there are some Nationalist soldiers entering the country. They watch for these too.'

'I can imagine they do,' Carradine murmured grimly. He rose to his knees and peered into the pale wash of moonlight directly ahead. He could just make out the stretch of coastline about three hundred yards away with the white lines of breakers which crashed on hidden reefs guarding any approach. He had to admit that Ts'ai Luan had chosen a particularly rugged part of land on which to attempt to beach the junk. As far as he was able to see in the dimness, there was no suitable landing place. Small as the junk was, it would require a narrow stretch of sand or shingle on which to ground.

The girl busied herself with the sail and a moment later it came rattling down at his feet. He glanced at her in surprise. 'They sometimes have searchlights to help them pick up fishing vessels that come close to the shore,' she explained. 'The sail would give us away at once if there are any men looking out on the top of the cliffs.'

'How do you intend to get ashore?' Carradine narrowed his eyes, searching the area. As far as he was able to see there was nothing but bare rock rising sheer from the water.

'We take the small boat. Then we shall have to climb.' She pointed. 'I'll lead the way. There is a route up the cliff which I've followed several times. The patrols will not be expecting anyone to climb at that point.'

'All right. If you say so.' He felt a little dubious, but the die had now been cast and he had no alternative but to go through with this. Checking that the Luger was firmly fastened inside the holster, he made his way along the deck and helped the girl lower the small boat over the other side. Twenty seconds later they had cast off, the tide carrying the frail boat shoreward at an alarming rate. He heard the girl shout something over the crashing roar of the breakers, then they slid miraculously between two gaping teeth of rock which thrust themselves out of the water on either side of them, either pinnacle capable of tearing the bottom out of the boat in a single instant. Moments later they entered an area of calm water and he let his breath sigh out in a long, heavy exhalation of relief — he had been quite unaware that he had stopped breathing — and hurriedly pulled hard on the oar, sending the boat towards the narrow inlet towards which the girl pointed.

'Once we're in there, I'll go first,' she called to him, her head close to his. 'Then follow me up.'

There was no time for any more. The boat was swinging almost broadside against the rocky bastion of the cliff.

From the corner of his eye he saw Ts'ai Luan climb nimbly onto the edge of the boat, then jump for the stretch of smooth rock scarcely three feet in width. Almost at once she began to climb. Without waiting he jumped, staggered a little, then caught his balance, felt for the surface of the narrow ledge immediately above him, and pulled himself up onto it beside the girl.

Lifting his head, he stared above him and gauged the distance to the top, estimating it to be about a hundred feet, possibly a little more. In places it appeared to be a sheer climb with neither handhold nor foothold in sight, yet the girl did not seem unduly disturbed by the prospect. She smiled up at him in the pale moonlight. 'Once we reach the top, the going is much easier,' she said philosophically.

'I certainly can't imagine it being any worse,' he agreed.

The first twenty feet were relatively easy. Out-thrusting boulders provided excellent handholds, but after that the going was much harder. He could understand how the girl had been so sure that the patrol would not be expecting anyone to climb

108

this way. How the girl was managing he did not know. As surely as a mountain goat, she found the almost invisible holds, waiting for him as he struggled up. There was a broader ledge some twenty feet from the top where they rested for a little while. From below, it had been completely invisible.

Ts'ai Luan gestured towards a rock at their backs, then up to where the shadowy edge was lined in the blurred outline against the faint glimmer of the night sky. She leaned forward, mouth close to his ear, the faint perfume of her dark hair in his nostrils. 'There is another ledge about five feet from the top, narrower than this. I will go up first. Keep close behind me.'

He nodded to show that he had understood. Stretching up, she hooked her fingers around a narrow outcrop of rock, climbing easily. Carradine waited until she had reached the ledge she had indicated, then began the final ascent. He felt like a fly on a windowpane, hanging there suspended more than a hundred feet above the frothing water. Ts'ai Luan had made the ledge. Dimly, he made out the pale blur of her face looking down at him. She had grasped a thick root which grew out of the solid rock with her left hand. Now she bent her knees and held her right hand down to him.

'Give me your hand,' she said urgently.

Feeling a trifle foolish, thinking incongruously that the positions should have been reversed, yet knowing that she had performed this climb many times before, he hung on with his right hand and lifted his left. She caught his wrist firmly as he wormed his way up. Then completely without warning, the two-inch-wide ledge beneath his feet crumbled. Before he was aware of what was happening he was swinging helplessly in mid-air, his chest striking painfully against the razor-sharp rocks. Madly, he flailed with his toe and free hand to find a fresh hold. This was surely the end, he thought desperately. The girl would have to release her hold on his wrist or be pulled off the ledge by his weight.

'Let go!' he shouted harshly. 'Or you'll be — '

'No!' Her voice came back to him from

above. 'Keep hold.'

The grip on his wrist tightened a fraction and then, incredibly, with an effort of which he had never believed her to be capable, the girl slowly straightened her legs, lifting all of his thirteen stone ten with her. His protruding toes found a narrow crack in the rocks a few seconds later and he thrust his boots into it, catching hold. Then with a heave he was over the edge of the ridge, lying on his chest, the breath rasping painfully in his lungs.

'You are all right?' He found her looking down at him, concern on her face.

Numbly, he nodded his head slowly. 'I don't know how you managed to do that,' he said hoarsely, 'but thanks. You saved my life.'

She smiled. 'You forget that I worked with an acrobatic troupe inside China. I'm used to it.'

'Sorry.' Carradine recalled the manner in which she had swung from one building to the next that morning. 'I guess I forgot.'

Noiselessly, and with infinite caution, they climbed to the top of the cliff and peered out into the darkness that lay beyond. Carradine remained quite still, searching about with eyes and ears, alert for the faintest sound, the slightest movement, all of his senses concentrated on watching for danger. There was nothing. Tall, rugged boulders lay strewn just beyond the rim of rock and some distance away where the darkness was less absolute than close at hand, the ground was broken up by patches of scrub, and he thought he could just make out a narrow road like a pale grey scar running through the countryside.

'There doesn't seem to be anyone about,' whispered the girl softly. 'Now we must hurry. We have a long way to go before dawn.'

★ ★ ★

It was almost three o'clock in the morning when they ran into trouble. For almost four hours they had made their way south-west without incident, the girl finding her way unerringly across rough country, following some track known only

112

to her. As they were climbing up a steep valley head, with the girl in the lead, she suddenly stopped and motioned Carradine down. Gradually, every movement controlled, she slid back to where he crouched.

'What is it?' he asked in a faint whisper. 'Somebody there?'

'A patrol,' she whispered back. 'I'm not sure how many men there are but they're coming this way.'

Cautiously, they moved back among the boulders, two shadows among other shadows. Now Carradine could hear the sound of the advancing patrol. They were making no secret of their presence so it seemed highly unlikely they were anticipating trouble.

There were only half a dozen of them, moving forward in a loose, strung-out bunch, rifles over their shoulders, faces invisible beneath the sloppy caps they wore. There was nothing organised or methodical about the way they moved and they talked loudly among themselves as they passed the huge boulders behind which Carradine and the girl crouched. They were still in sight, a slowly dwindling blur in the darkness, the sound of their boots ringing on the rocks when they came out of the hiding place and struck off over the spur of the hill. On the other side they entered an area of rice fields, the first signs of cultivation they had encountered.

'We are only a few miles from Canton now,' whispered Ts'ai Luan. 'We must be very careful.'

Soon they entered a small cluster of trees. Making as little noise as possible, they moved through them. On the far side, Carradine paused to examine the moonlit ground which lay spread out before them. The paddy fields were now way off to his right. On their left the ground was rougher, more broken. It looked difficult stuff to cross, but unhesitatingly the girl pointed in that direction. Her voice broke in on his thoughts.

'That way now. There are workers in the huts on the edge of the paddy fields, and sometimes they have dogs. We may be able to slip past the sleeping men in the huts but the dogs would be able to scent us within minutes and raise the alarm.'

Carradine nodded dubiously. He edged forward, then paused as the girl said tightly: 'There's someone coming behind us.'

'Are you sure?' Carradine listened intently but heard nothing other than the faint sighing of the wind through the bending branches overhead.

'I'm sure,' she murmured. She moved away from him and in a pale shaft of moonlight which filtered through the leaves, he saw the glint of the knife in her hand. Instinctively, he closed his fingers about the butt of the Luger, easing it out.

Then he heard the stealthy movement in the undergrowth. Crouching down, he waited, hoping that the girl had learned how to take care of herself with that knife. He held the gun uncertainly in his hand, eyes narrowed down to merc slits as she watched for the first sign of movement. Slowly, the noise of the men in the brush increased. He could see no sign of the girl, and did not dare call out to her. He swore softly under his breath. In hand-to-hand combat such as this promised to be, a girl was an extra disadvantage, no matter how capable she might be. It meant he would have to keep an eye on her as well as on himself.

Then he saw the bushes part less than ten yards away and a second later two men came out into the small clearing, looking about them alertly. He tensed as he saw that they were both dressed in some kind of uniform. They must have spotted them from a distance, as they had crossed open country and moved stealthily behind to take them by surprise.

For what seemed an eternity the men waited, heads cocked to one side, listening for some sound of them. When they heard nothing, they conferred together for a moment in low voices, then split up, moving around both sides of the clearing. They were watchful and wary, their heads turning from side to side as they advanced. Clearly they were taking no chances on being ambushed. The rifles were held tightly in their fists in an attitude of menace.

Crouched there, holding his breath until it hurt in his chest, Carradine wondered if this was more of Kellaway's doing; if the other had sent a warning message to his Communist masters, telling them what had happened — that he had left alone, possibly suspecting something. It might also explain that patrol they had bumped into earlier.

The nearer of the two men was now less than three yards away, edging closer. He tensed. Would the other get close enough to him so that he might use the gun at an extremely close range? The sound of a gunshot, unless muffled in some way, would carry for miles in the night stillness. Carradine decided that he could not afford to take any chances on the other passing him without noticing him. As soon as the man was near enough he would shoot to kill and hope for the best. Whether he could distract the other man's attention long enough for the girl to use the knife, he did not know.

Controlling his breathing, he got one leg under him. Five seconds passed, then ten. The man drew alongside. With a sudden convulsive surge of motion, Carradine hurled himself upright and thrust the barrel of the Luger hard against the man's side, his other arm snaking around the neck. Pressing the weapon as far as he could into the rough tunic, he squeezed the trigger once. The recoil of the heavy pistol slammed hard against his ribs, almost breaking the bone. The man uttered a thin, strangled bleat of sound that died virtually instantly, then slumped heavily against him, a great hole in his side. With an effort, Carradine retained his stranglehold around the dead man's neck, holding him up, swinging him around so that he formed a human shield as the second soldier whirled sharply, levelling the rifle in his direction.

Before the other had a chance to pull the trigger, a slim shape rose up from the ground at his back. There was a faint gleam of moonlight on cold steel as the knife flashed downward into the soldier's back just below the neck. For a moment the other remained incredibly upright. Then he collapsed inertly forward and lay stretched out on the ground, the girl standing over him. Calmly, she withdrew the knife.

'He is dead,' she said softly.

Carradine forced a quick laugh. His throat felt suddenly dry. 'My, but you're a bloodthirsty little she-cat, aren't you?'

'I don't understand,' she said, coming close to him.

He shook himself. 'Never mind. We'd better move on quickly. There may be others in the vicinity and when these two don't come back, they'll move in on us and maybe try to cut us off.'

Ts'ai Luan nodded in agreement. Together they moved off through the dense scrub.

★　★　★

Seated in the same plush chair beneath the large photograph of Mao Tse Tung, Lung Chan surveyed the two men who stood before him at the side of the long table. The bland features did not reflect the deep flame of anger that stirred and moved inside him. Only the pudgy fingers, tight on the table's edge, betrayed something of his thoughts as he said coldly: 'It would appear that certain of my orders have not been carried out. My information is that, in spite of what I commanded, there were two further attempts on the life of the British agent yesterday. However, both of them failed — but that is not the point I wish to bring to your attention.'

One after the other, he examined the faces of the men standing before him. He knew that inwardly, in spite of their appearance of calm, they were both extremely disturbed, possibly frightened men. Both were directly responsible for the way in which their agents inside the British colony operated. It had been their duty to ensure that his orders had been carried out to the letter the moment the previous day's conference had broken up.

'Apparently the last attempt failed because this man — Carradine — was aided by someone unknown to us. This is a grave blow and must be rectified at once.'

'That will be done, General,' murmured Chin Wang. 'There is sometimes difficulty in contacting — '

'Enough!' roared the other. He hammered with his clenched fist on the table. 'I want no further excuses. Already, this mission is completely out of hand. I received further disturbing information two hours ago. The Englishman, Kellaway, who has been working for us inside Hong Kong, reports that Carradine did not leave with our two men. When they returned to Kellaway's house, Carradine was no longer there. The fact that he had taken the papers which had been prepared for him indicates that he had decided to take some other route into China. We therefore have to face the possibility that someone is helping him. This makes our task a little more difficult than it would normally have been.'

'Perhaps,' Chin Wang spoke a trifle hesitantly, 'if this is the case, it makes our task of finding him almost impossible. China is a very large country, and by now he could have landed anywhere along the coast. No doubt he is suitably disguised.'

'Of course he will be disguised, you fool,' roared Lung Chan savagely. 'Do you expect him to enter China as an Englishman?'

'Of course not, General,' mumbled the other apologetically. He lowered his glance from the other's face.

Lung Chan tightened his thick lips momentarily. He now knew that his early instincts about this man had been fundamentally correct. The other was incompetent and a fool. He would soon have to be relieved of his post. When the time came for this, it would also be necessary to see that he did not live to speak of anything he had learned while he had been Head of the State Security Division. He had never really liked the other. It would give him the greatest personal pleasure to supervise his ultimate demise.

'The task is by no means impossible,' Lung Chan went on blandly a moment later. 'He will come to China for one purpose only: to discover the whereabouts of Chao Lin. That will be his sole concern. We hold Chao Lin and very soon, like the fly of the Western proverb, this man Carradine will walk into our trap.'

'Then a trap has been prepared for him?' inquired Chin Wang politely.

'Naturally. That has all been taken care of. There is, however, the question of the Englishman, Kellaway. He is no longer of any value to us. He knows far too much and must be eliminated.' His eyes rested on Chin Wang's face and noticed the faint crease of the brows above the eyes. 'That will be your responsibility. As he may now be considered a threat to the security of the state.'

'I shall arrange it at once,' murmured the other. He felt he had got off lightly. Perhaps if he made certain that Kellaway died within the next few hours his previous mistake might be, if not forgotten, at least overlooked.

'That is all for the moment,' said Lung Chan decisively. 'I shall, however, require you to remain in your respective offices should I need you urgently. This matter is of such importance that it is being watched carefully by others.' He did not mention any names, withholding them deliberately for dramatic effect, but one look at the faces of the two men told him that they knew exactly who he was talking about.

★ ★ ★

The van which drove up to the front of the apartment looked like many hundreds

123

of others on the side streets of Hong Kong every day. The legend painted on the side said that it was from the telephone company. Kellaway experienced a faint sense of surprise as two men got out and came towards the door. He let the curtain fall into place as the bell rang.

The tall man showed his card. He smiled pleasantly. 'We have been asked to check every telephone in this district,' he said sibilantly. 'Please do not alarm yourself; there is nothing wrong. This is merely a periodic test we have to make now that there are so many on the island.'

Kellaway gave the card back and nodded. 'I suppose you had better come in then,' he said reluctantly. 'I hope this won't take too long, as there are several important calls I have to make.'

'Fifteen minutes at the most,' said the other. 'If you could just show us where it is.'

'Of course.' He led the way into the study and nodded towards the phone on his desk. 'This is the only one I have.'

'Thank you. The check is quite

straightforward, sir.'

The tall man lifted the phone from its plastic cradle, spun the dial several times, then nodded as if satisfied.

Kellaway walked over to the window and poured himself a stiff drink. This intrusion was the last thing he wanted just at this moment and it had been in his mind to refuse the men entry, using some excuse or other. Since Carradine had vanished the previous evening, just when everything seemed to have been going according to plan, he had felt shaken and disturbed. It had not been his fault at all, he told himself fiercely. Something must have happened while Carradine had been away checking over Chao Lin's office in the morning, although the other had not mentioned anything about it. Indeed, during the whole of the afternoon while they had been at the plastic surgeon's making the temporary alterations to his face, and later when his photograph had been taken downtown for the papers, he had acted quite normally. There had been nothing to give him cause to suspect that the other would not go through with the plan they had discussed together.

Yet the fact that he had gone, taking the papers with him, almost certainly meant that somehow the other had become suspicious of him. Yet how in God's name could that have happened? There was no one in Hong Kong, apart from the handful of Red Dragon agents he knew, who could have told Carradine anything at all. He had made absolutely certain that no one else knew of the double role he had been playing for the past few years. So what could have happened?

Tossing the drink down, he tried to go over in his mind all the details since he had met Carradine at the airport. The bomb attack on the car had surely been sufficiently reliably carried out to be realistic, and he had deliberately knocked himself out on the dashboard to make it absolutely convincing. He poured a second drink. So it all boiled down to the inescapable fact that the fault lay with the operatives of the Red Dragon themselves and not with him at all. He felt a little easier in his mind as this thought occurred to him, clinging to it as a drowning man to a straw; for there would certainly be questions asked in Canton now that they knew what had happened. Awkward questions if General Lung Chan did not believe his defence.

He ran a shaking hand over his forehead and stared down at the faint sheen of sweat on his flesh. He felt suddenly cold. Why the hell had he got himself mixed up in this business, anyway? At first it had been the sense of adventure, rather than the money — and then both. Once Chao Lin had been kidnapped, however, the full precariousness of his own position had been borne home to him. More than once, he had considered asking London to relieve him of his duties here, to be transferred to some other part of the world, as far away from Hong Kong as was humanly possible. Two things had stopped him each time he had tried to send the wire.

Firstly, he knew that whatever the answer from London may be, he would have to remain here until someone else was sent out and the Hong Kong station re-established and the mystery of Chao

Lin's disappearance satisfactorily settled. Secondly, possibly more important still, he knew with an unshakeable certainty that no matter where he went, the arm of the Red Dragon and its vengeance could reach clear across the world and that at some time or other, retribution would catch up with him.

He glanced at his watch. It was almost eleven o'clock. Another twenty minutes and he would have to put through his routine call to his contact in the city. He felt the knowing touch of fear in his stomach sharpen into actual physical pain. Whatever happened, that call had to go through. The Red Dragon insisted on punctuality in this matter. He knew that if he was even a minute early or late with his call, there would be no answer at the other end, and very soon, someone would come out to see why he had failed to get in touch.

The two men were still busy with the phone and he stood idly by the window, staring down into the street. He wanted to relax, but his turbulent thoughts would not allow him to do so. Every dammed thing about this whole business seemed to be getting out of hand. Before he knew where he was, London would start getting suspicious and then there would be hell to pay. Trying to play off one side against the other was like walking a tightrope blindfolded.

The voice of the taller Chinese broke in on his troubled thoughts. 'I'm sure you will find that the telephone operates quite satisfactorily now, sir.' They began packing their tools away in the small leather bag on the table.

'Thank you,' Kellaway said curtly. He followed them to the door and closed it behind them. He would have much preferred it if the authorities had given him some advanced warning of this visit by their workmen. The trouble was, he reflected, that these days they did not seem to care about the private rights of the citizen. It was well known that the Chinese did not like the British and often went out of their way to make them realise this by making life as irksome as possible, while still appearing courteous and civil on the surface.

He checked with his watch again. Another five minutes before the call was due. From the window, he watched the telephone van drive away. The street was quiet again.

The next five minutes seemed interminable. If only he could get his mind into some kind of order and think straight again. Damn that fellow Carradine, he thought fiercely. He got nervously to his feet, poured another drink, and stood with it in his hand, glancing at the watch on his left wrist every fifteen seconds; watching the red second hand drag itself slowly around the circular face. If Carradine had somehow managed to get into China, there might be no stopping him. Still, he consoled himself, Chinese Intelligence was far better than he had ever imagined before he had come out here to Hong Kong. That was where the British Secret Service had made their big mistake, in underestimating the enemy. If they did not watch their step, it would eventually prove to be their undoing.

Draining his glass, he went over to the desk and sat down. He could feel the perspiration forming in tiny pools under his arms and in little beads on his forehead as he tried to visualise the orders he would receive from his contact.

Now it was time. Picking up the phone from the plastic cradle, he held it to his ear and began to dial the number with the forefinger of his left hand. The phone clicked as he spun the dial. As it spun back into place after the last digit, there was a louder crack than usual; but Kellaway heard only the fractional beginning of the sound. Inside the round mouthpiece, there was a faint puff of smoke following the slight explosion. The thin sliver of steel, no more than two inches in length, pierced the roof of his mouth and lanced into his brain in microseconds.

5

The Fuse Is Lit

Carradine awoke lazily. For long moments he lay on his back staring up at the unfamiliar ceiling, struggling to recall where he was; then memory came flooding back with a rush and he swung his legs to the floor, getting to his feet. The sun through the nearby window was already high in the sky and hot. Two minutes later, as he pulled on his nondescript clothing, the door opened and Ts'ai Luan came into the small room.

'I let you sleep on through the morning,' she said brightly. 'You were so tired after the journey last night that it seemed a pity to wake you.'

'Did any of your friends manage to discover anything about the Red Dragon? Where they took your uncle?'

'They say that some men brought a prisoner into Canton more than a week ago, just after I left China. It may have been my uncle, but they could not be sure. He was well guarded.'

'My guess is that it was him. At least, it means that he's probably still alive.'

The girl's face assumed a serious expression. 'I hope that is true,' she said soberly. 'The Red Dragon will undoubtedly torture him to learn as many secrets as they can. But once they believe he can tell them nothing more, they will certainly kill him.'

That was a possibility which had been in Carradine's thoughts for some days. The Chinese had short shrift as far as traitors went. Once a man was of no further use, they destroyed him. He only hoped that they might get to Chao Lin in time. He felt a little ashamed to realise that he was more concerned with the military secrets locked away inside the girl's uncle's head than with his personal safety.

It had been shortly before dawn when they had finally reached the outskirts of Canton. The girl had led the way unerringly through the shanties on the edge of the city. The moon had been low by that time and there had been only the stars lighting the heavens as they had moved through quiet, darkened streets and alleys, eventually reaching this building, where she had knocked softly on the door to be admitted by a giant of a man with a cruel hawk-like face and a great bald head which had glistened in the faint candlelight. This, she had told him, was Tai Fan, a deaf-mute and the leader of the acrobatic troupe with which she worked.

In spite of the deep-seated weariness in his body, an hour had been spent in discussing the situation with the other members of the troupe, three men and two girls. From the conversation it had become apparent that, as in Russia, circus folk occupied a privileged position inside Communist China, being able to move without question throughout most of the country. Playing as they did all over China, their comings and goings were accepted without reserve and he could not have hoped for a better source of information. How far they could all be trusted, he was not quite sure. But now that he was inside China, he would have to play it all by ear.

'Is there any way of getting further information?'

'Perhaps. There is to be a performance tonight. It is rumoured that General Lung Chan will be there. He is the Head of the Red Dragon in Canton.'

'Lung Chan.' Carradine turned the name over in his mind. It meant nothing to him. 'What sort of a man is he?'

'He is the Devil himself.' The girl looked at him sharply. 'He has men everywhere and they say that whoever goes into that room at the top of the Red Dragon Headquarters never comes out — alive.'

'He sounds like a pleasant character,' Carradine said dryly. 'Most likely a very difficult man to get at.'

'Surely you are not so foolish as to think that you can kidnap him and make him talk, or maybe hold him as hostage for my uncle.'

'It's an idea,' Carradine murmured thoughtfully.

'Then you must forget it at once.' Ts'ai Luan was perfectly serious. 'It would be committing suicide. No one can get to

135

him. He is the most feared and powerful man in southern China. Only on very rare occasions does he leave their headquarters, and then he is accompanied by a strong bodyguard. He would not be easy to kill.'

Carradine was beginning to realise the full extent of what he was up against. 'And the Headquarters building? Can we get inside without being seen?'

The girl hesitated, then nodded slowly, thoughtfully. 'That may be possible,' she agreed. 'The main entrance is well guarded, but at the back there is a single window which can be opened from the outside.' She paused and went on quietly: 'Unfortunately it is on the third floor. There are no others.'

Carradine cocked an eye at her. 'Then that rules that out. More than likely they have men, maybe even dogs, patrolling the area when they have an important prisoner held there. Gaining entry would have to be quick. We could never manage to get ladders in place, even if we could lay our hands on them.'

'There may be a much better way than

using ladders,' said the girl, smiling enigmatically. 'But we'll talk about this later. In the meantime, the others will be trying to gather further information about my uncle. We must first discover exactly where they are keeping him. Tai Fan knows the inside of the Headquarters building as well as anyone outside of the Red Dragon. He will guide us if we do get inside.'

Carradine had a breakfast of rice and some kind of dry fig with tea in an eggshell-thin cup. He was ravenously hungry and had hoped that the food might be as good as he had heard that it could be in China. He was not disappointed. The tea had just the right tang to it to titivate the palate and the rice had been prepared with tiny pieces of chopped meat and vegetables, which were delicious.

Punctually at ten o'clock, Ts'ai Luan came in with two other members of the troupe. Her eyes were strangely hard and shrewd, but her tone was mild as she said: 'Tei Shin reports that the Red Dragon are questioning a man today at their Head-quarters, a man answering the description

137

of my uncle. He was there to arrange for the performances this evening and saw two guards take the prisoner into the lift which goes straight to the room at the top. That is where they hold their secret conferences, make their plans and also interrogate their prisoners.'

'Then whatever happens, it will have to be tonight,' Carradine said decisively. 'Chao Lin is an old man. Even if he wishes, he could not withstand torture for very long. He would have to talk.'

'You are afraid, of course, for the secrets he has in his head concerning your organisation,' murmured the girl softly. She seated herself in the chair near the window where she could watch the street below.

'Not particularly.' Carradine shook his head. 'If they had been after any of our secrets they could have taken them when they kidnapped your uncle and destroyed the Hong Kong station. I'm much more interested in what Chao Lin has discovered about a secret weapon which he believes your scientists have devised and were on the point of testing.' He sat back.

With an effort, he forced some of the tension out of his voice and relaxed his body. 'But if you think there is a way of getting inside the place, then all is not lost. We may yet rescue your uncle before they decide he has told them everything he knows. But we need a plan. It will have to be carried out with split-second timing.'

'I understand.' She said something to the two men in Cantonese, speaking so rapidly that it was impossible for Carradine to follow her. They gave brief nods and left the room. 'I have told them to keep a watch on the Red Dragon Headquarters, to check on the guards and also make sure that no prisoners are taken away. We must accept the possibility that by now, Lung Chan knows you have reached China and will make an attempt to rescue my uncle. He will have taken additional precautions to prevent this and also to capture you.' She rose lithely to her feet. 'Now we will discuss the best way of getting into the building. It will not be easy, but if we are to succeed, it is essential that we should know what we are doing.'

Carradine grinned at her. 'Sometimes I think that London would have done better if they had put you in charge of the Hong Kong station.'

More tea came as they took each piece of information they had, checked it, dissected it, and then went through everything again. An hour passed; then another. Gradually, a plan was formulated. At the end of that time, Carradine realised that Ts'ai Luan possessed an extremely quick and agile mind. Ruthless at times, she could also cut through all of the deadwood which so often surrounded a plan such as this and get to the very heart of the problem. Her knowledge of Canton came from several years of keen and perceptive experience, almost as though her life there had all been the leading up to this moment.

'This afternoon, Tai Fan will draw us a plan of the building. It will be accurate in every detail except for the topmost floor. That,' she headed apologetically, 'is something no one outside the Red Dragon has ever seen and lived to tell of. However, it is almost certain that my uncle will be kept prisoner in the basement. They have cells for their prisoners.'

'You realise, of course, what will happen to us if we should fail.'

She nodded her head slowly. 'They will kill us all,' she murmured simply.

Grimly, Carradine added: 'First they will make certain that we suffer. It will not be a quick and easy death.'

Ts'ai Luan held her head high, her dark eyes flashing. 'Do you think I care what those Communist pigs do to me? We are fighting for freedom. If we are to die, then so be it. But there will be others to take our place. The battle will go on until all of China is free.'

'You're an extremely brave girl,' Carradine said. He looked down at the calm, beautiful face, the dark lashes fringing the slanted eyes; the soft, pale swell of the cheeks and the red lips, parted a little. Acting on impulse, he placed his arms around her waist, pulled her to him and felt the warmth of her body, alive and vital, against his. Bending his head, he kissed her hard on the lips and felt her respond, her arms tightening around his neck. She remained in his arms for a long moment, as though afraid to let him go; as if he was her only sane contact in this crazy, frightening world, this dark existence. Then she freed herself and stepped back, her eyes veiled.

'Perhaps I was wrong to do that,' he said softly.

Her lips curved into a smile. 'I think I wanted you to do it,' she answered, equally softly. Then, in a matter-of-fact tone: 'There seems to be so little time for love in this world today.'

★　★　★

At seven o'clock that evening, the girl came for him. She was dressed in a silk tunic, buttoned tightly at the neck and a short, pleated skirt of the same material. Her long, black hair hung down in a pony-tail, knotted with a white ribbon.

'We're ready to go now, Steve,' she said quietly. 'You must take the map of the Red Dragon Headquarters with you. When the show is finished, we shall not return here but drive to the outskirts of Canton so that we may watch the building, ready to choose the best moment to put our plan into action.'

'Do you think it will be safe for me to go with you?' he asked. 'After all, if anyone questions me, my Chinese isn't sufficiently fluent to fool them for long.'

'No one will question you,' answered the girl. She smiled brightly. 'You will join us in our performance. There, at least, you will be safe.'

'But that's out of the question,' Carradine protested vehemently. 'I know nothing of acrobatics. The first mistake and it would give the game away completely.'

'You've no need to worry,' the girl assured him. 'The others know exactly what to do. Just follow me. We can all cover for you.'

'I only hope you're right.' Carradine sounded dubious.

'Trust me,' she said reassuringly. 'This isn't the first time we've done this.'

Carradine raised his brows quizzically.

Ts'ai Luan looked up at his face. Her features were suddenly alive. 'We used to smuggle political refugees out of China and often this was the only way to do it. Those fools never questioned our troupe. We have our own truck in which we carry our props and moved from town to town. It was easy to take them under their very noses.'

Carradine said thoughtfully: 'Then I hope you're just as successful this time. We're playing for even higher stakes now.'

★ ★ ★

The theatre was somewhere in the centre of Canton, set back a little from the main street. Standing in the wings, Carradine felt the muscles of his stomach tighten involuntarily and forced his fingers to relax by his sides. Around the edge of the thick, heavy curtain, he could just make out the first few rows of the audience, a sea of grey from which no features were distinguishable. The interior differed in only a few respects from any medium-sized variety theatre in one of the provincial towns of England. The trappings were a little less luxurious and the spotlights fainter and more erratic, a fact for which he was extremely grateful. Ts'ai Luan came up beside him, slipped her hand into his, and squeezed it tightly.

'There is General Lung Chan.' She motioned towards the box on the far side of the theatre.

Carradine narrowed his eyes and gazed towards the huge figure seated in the centre of the box with a sprinkling of uniformed men on either side of him. There were too, he noticed, a couple of armed guards at the rear of the general's box, the faint light shining off the snub barrels of their submachine-guns.

Evidently, even here, Lung Chan was taking no unnecessary chances.

Carradine smiled grimly to himself. He could visualise the kind of life the other was forced to live because of his position. Men who wielded power in China — particularly vicious, cruel men such as Lung Chan — had to be on watch every second of the day. In spite of the iron hand which held the vast majority of the teeming millions in check, there would always be some waiting to kill him: people with relatives who had been murdered and tortured on his orders, and others who disagreed violently with the present regime, for not all of the enemies of the Communist state were huddled together on the island of Formosa, protected by the heavy guns of the American Navy. There were bound to be some inside China itself — fanatics, just biding their time.

While the act preceding them went through their routine, he spent the time studying the other's face, filing the details away inside his brain. The porcine eyes were almost lost in the flabby mountain of flesh, the mouth a thin gash below the nostrils, opening and closing spasmodically as he watched the stage. Almost casually, as he watched this dreadful man, he wondered just how much longer he would remain alive — how much longer the man would remain in his job, even if he were not assassinated by some fanatic. Naturally, like all others in high positions, Lung Chan would possess a tremendous will to survive, a desperate need to reach the top of his murderous profession. Undoubtedly, he would have been one of the men who had lived and fought with the Communist clique when they had driven out the Nationalist forces under Chiang Kai-shek: a man who could be trusted to carry out all orders passed on to him; a man who held human life extremely cheaply, and who would murder to gain his own ends. The pudgy hands rested lightly on the edge of the box, clasped almost in prayer, blood-stained hands with the deaths of God alone knew how many victims on them. As he watched the other closely from beneath lowered lids, Carradine knew that of all of the men he had met in this deadly Cold War game, General Lung Chan was one he would kill without compunction, without a qualm on his conscience if ever the need and the opportunity arose. Such a man would have found an ideal place working with Hitler, Stalin or Tojo, he reflected idly; a man for whom mass murder was a common, every-day occurrence.

Without turning his head, he said softly: 'Does he return to their Headquarters after the performance?'

'Almost invariably.' Ts'ai Luan smiled

tightly. 'Perhaps he realises, as no one else does, that it is not safe for him to be out in the city after dark. There are too many shadows from which a bullet or a knife could come.'

The act on the stage finished their performance. There was polite clapping from the audience. Once again, Carradine experienced the momentary tightness in his chest as if his breath was stopped up somewhere between his lungs and his throat. Then they were out on the stage and there was no time to think of the watching audience or of Lung Chan up there in the box, staring down at them. He forced himself only to concentrate on what was happening immediately around him, knowing that he had to devote all of his attention to following the actions of the various members of the troupe. For the first time, he was thankful for the grounding in gymnastics which he had been forced to carry out during his training.

All in all, he found it easier than he had imagined. On the way to the theatre the girl had given him some idea of their routine, which consisted for the most part of individual or double acts, somersaulting over the huge flag which Tai Fan waved across almost the entire length and breadth of the stage, timing one's movements with those of the others. The climax of the act was the most difficult as far as he was concerned: a human pyramid in the very centre of the stage with twin spotlights playing over them.

Ts'ai Luan moved quickly to him and whispered: 'Stand quite still.'

Before he could reply, she had grasped his hands and vaulted up onto his shoulders. Out of the corner of his eye, he saw that the others had done the same and were moving slowly towards the giant figure of Tai Fan. He advanced with them from one side, stood unmoving beside the other while Ts'ai Luan scrambled lightly upward, and was caught by the arms of two other members balanced seemingly precariously on Tai Fan's huge shoulders. Seconds later, his right hand was caught in a grip of steel and he felt himself swung off his seat as the latter held them all off the ground.

There came a tumult of applause from the audience. For perhaps ten seconds the pose was held, then Ts'ai Luan dropped lightly to her feet in front of him and he found himself lowered to the ground, with Tai Fan grinning hugely all over his round moon-face. As he followed the others off the stage into the dimness of the wings, Carradine threw a quick, furtive glance up towards the box and saw that Lung Chan was politely clapping his hands. He let his breath go from his lungs in a soundless side of relief. There had been no suspicion on the other's part. *We've made it,* thought Carradine. *I really think we made it with no trouble.* The tense lines around his eyes and mouth relaxed.

Ts'ai Luan was smiling broadly as she took his arm. 'There, that wasn't too difficult, was it?'

'Not really. Although there were moments when I thought someone might become suspicious.'

'We should have you in the act always,' murmured one of the others in slow, deliberate words, so that Carradine was able to understand.

'I think I'll stay in my own particular kind of business. I find it less precarious.'

They made their way down to the row of shabby dressing rooms. There was half an hour before the show ended and it would look extremely suspicious if they were to leave before it was over. Until then, they simply had to kill time and remain inconspicuous.

Carradine spent almost a quarter of an hour going over the map which Tai Fan had drawn of the interior of the Red Dragon Headquarters. This was indeed a great help to them, he thought inwardly, studying it closely — having someone who knew the inside of that place, even if he knew nothing of the topmost floor. With a man such as Tai Fan with them, how could they possibly fail? he reflected. A mountain of a man — strong, seemingly indestructible; he was going to be invaluable.

'As you will see,' said Ts'ai Luan, glancing over his shoulder at the map spread out on the cheap dressing table, 'the window I told you about opens into this corridor here. At the end of it, there are stairs leading down through the remaining floors to the basement. At this time of night it is unlikely that these corridors will be patrolled. They will have men, and possibly dogs, in the grounds. The building itself is situated well away from any others for obvious reasons.'

Carradine tightened his lips. He could well imagine what some of these reasons were. Not only those of security, although they would figure high on the list, but also so that the screams of the tortured would not disturb other people in nearby houses. 'But there will be some sort of staff still working there?' he said, looking up.

She nodded. 'They work twenty-four hours a day there,' she said harshly. 'That is one place in Canton which never sleeps. The business of security and espionage goes on all the time.'

'So we shall have to be prepared to silence anyone who may come along.' Carradine said the words half to himself, expecting no answer. 'I suppose it could be worse if, as you say, they will not be expecting us to get in this way.' He prodded the drawing with his forefinger, pointing out the window to the rear of the building.

He folded the map carefully and stuffed it into his voluminous pocket. The weight of the Luger nuzzling against his stomach reminded him that he was still carrying the weapon. He took it out, checked the clip, then thrust it back into the butt of the gun, clicking the safety catch on. He was about to replace a pistol in his belt when the girl caught his hand.

'Better not to take that along with you,' she said softly, warningly. 'This will have to be a silent affair. That will make far too much noise. A knife will be the best weapon to use — quick and quiet.'

Carradine hesitated for a moment. He hated to be parted with the gun. It had been his constant companion for as long as he could remember. He was used to it; felt oddly naked without it. Yet he was forced to see the logic of her words. If they did run into trouble, it would almost certainly be fighting at close quarters, and the heavy pistol was useless for that. But what if they had to silence a man at long range?'

Almost as if she was divining his thoughts, Ts'ai Luan said: 'Tai Fan is an expert knife-thrower, Steve. He can kill a man without a sound at forty paces. Make no mistake about that. Leave the gun in the truck.'

'Very well. Anything you say.'

Now it was just a question of sitting out the minutes, listening to the occasional bursts of applause in the distance, the sounds of the other artists on the programme returning to their rooms. Sitting in that small, dingy room, Carradine tried to imagine what had happened during the day to Chao Lin. Had they already finished with him? Was he dead even at that moment, his body being quickly and professionally disposed of so as to arouse no suspicion? Somehow he doubted it. In spite of his age, Chao Lin was a professional man who knew the risks he had been facing when he had been given the job as head of the Hong Kong station, and the fact that he had proved so useful to the British and had discovered so much about the Communists was a telling reflection on his capabilities as a spy. It was unusual, for the rough kind of torture meted out by men of the Red Dragon would have much effect on such a man at the beginning. One who knew all of the tricks could keep the pot boiling for a long time, giving many pieces of information, some true, some false, and all having to be verified before the enemy could be sure.

One thing was certain: Chao Lin would not reveal the secrets he had discovered, knowing that once news of his kidnapping had reached London, another agent would be sent out immediately to try to pick up the threads. Whether Chao Lin guessed that anyone might be so rash as to attempt to take him from the Red Dragon Headquarters was another matter, but he would certainly hold on for as long as he possibly could in the hope that a miracle might happen.

Carradine concentrated on getting as many details of the inside of the Headquarters into his mind as possible during the last few minutes. He discovered that the palms of his hands were wet and wiped them on the silken trousers he was wearing. Then he got up and stretched.

How Ts'ai Luan could possibly look so unconcerned at the prospect of the night's work, he did not know; yet there was not a line of worry on her calm, glowing features. The rest of the troupe made their preparations with care. Tai Fan had a trio of long-bladed throwing knives in his belt and at intervals, he took them out and ran the ball of his thumb along the keen blades, nodding in satisfaction.

There came a sudden chant from the distance. It was impossible to make out the individual words but the whole audience seemed to be repeating the name Mao Tse Tung over and over again in an endless rhythm.

'That's it,' said Ts'ai Luan softly. She came over to his side and looked up at him. 'Now we must go.'

They left by the small side door of the theatre, walking slowly. No hurry now! There was a small knot of people waiting outside, and a sprinkling of men in uniform among them. Carradine felt his heart jump, hammering, into the base of his throat. But the small crowd was evidently not waiting for them, and a few moments later they were through and making their way towards the waiting truck. He did not relax until they were driving slowly through the dark streets with the three-quarter moon riding over the tops of the building.

The truck was parked fifteen minutes later in a small alley, with the lights switched off. Now that they were on the outskirts of Canton, the streets were almost deserted. There was scarcely any traffic at all in sight and the few people who were out hurried by and did not give them a second look. Carradine guessed that with the huge squat building just in sight on the other side of the street, they knew from past experience that it was not wise to stop and ask questions of anyone in a car or truck. Only the army, or the Red Guard — a newly formed organisation inside China, or a few important people possessed vehicles of any kind.

'Now we must wait for a while,' murmured the girl. 'We made a wide detour to get here so it is possible that the general's car has already arrived.'

Carradine leaned forward and peered through the wide windscreen. There were still a great many lights still showing yellowly in the windows of the Headquarters building, but on the topmost floor, only pale glimmers where thick shutters had been drawn over the windows.

'There!' said one of the men in a sibilant hiss.

Carradine had been taking too much notice of the faint gleams of light on the top floor, wondering inwardly what went on there, to notice what might be happening down below. He lowered his hand swiftly, following the direction of the man's pointing finger.

Two dark figures had come into sight around the far corner of the building: guards with rifles over their shoulders. They were followed by three other shapes: huge, loping animals with flat skulls and powerful legs. Some kind of hunting dog very similar to a German Shepherd, Carradine reflected. Hell, it would be the end if they were caught by any of those. A knife would be of little use against such a creature. They looked as if they could savage a man within seconds of attacking him.

'They must have doubled the guards,' whispered the girl. 'Usually they have only one man and a dog. We will watch and check their movements before going in.'

Carradine nodded. It was only to be expected. Chao Lin was perhaps the biggest fish they had netted for some time and they would be taking no risks with him. Taking out the heavy Luger, he placed it in front of the truck, then sat back, only to feel something being thrust into his right hand. There was a touch of cold steel against his palm and fingers and he knew, without looking down, that it was one of Tai Fan's throwing knives. He grinned at the other, feeling the coldness in his face. It was some time since he had killed with a knife. He hoped that he had not lost all of his former skill.

Fifteen minutes passed, then half an hour. Carradine felt the tension beginning to grow until it stretched his nerves to breaking point. They had watched as the Chinese guards had circled the building and Carradine had noticed that they moved warily, keeping well away from the shadowy bushes which dotted the grounds. There wasn't anything sloppy about the way in which these two men kept watch. Almost certainly they had been specially briefed, had been warned to look out for trouble, and were taking no chances on being jumped from the shadows.

'Tai Fan will take care of the guards,' said Ts'ai Luan in a soft murmur.

'What about the dogs?'

'Don't worry about them. We have something which will stop them in their tracks.' She nodded towards one of the other men, who placed a hand inside the voluminous folds of his tunic and drew out a long bamboo pipe. Holding out his left hand, he showed the three tiny feathered darts to Carradine. 'These are tipped with a quick-acting poison which completely paralyses the muscular system,' Ts'ai Luan explained. 'It works within two seconds.'

'You seem to have thought of everything,' he said in admiration. 'The more I know about you, Ts'ai Luan, the more I'm certain that London should have put you in command of the station.'

She flashed him a quick smile, lowered her head to peer through the windscreen, then caught his arm, her fingers tightening convulsively. 'The guards have just gone around the rear of the corner. We have less than three minutes to get into position. Quickly!'

Carradine slid out of the truck and followed her across the empty street, onto the rough stretch of ground which separated the Red Dragon Headquarters from the road. The other men were vaguely seen shadows flitting soundlessly forward, the huge form of Tai Fan easily discernible until he had melted from sight among the bushes. Within two minutes of leaving the truck they had all crept out of sight. Carradine held his breath in his lungs. The haft of the knife was hard against his palm as he steadied himself.

The moon-flooded silence held for what seemed an eternity. Then it was broken by the sound of heavy footsteps approaching from the front of the building. The guards were returning on their monotonous circuit. Cautiously, Carradine lifted his head. He felt a tiny prickle of sweat on his forehead. There came the faint hiss of breath near his right ear. 'They're coming! Just keep out of sight and leave this to the others.'

The dark shapes of the men emerged from the corner of the building. The dogs were just visible a little distance behind them. They continued forward at the same steady pace, oblivious to the fact that both would be dead before they had drawn another five breaths into their lungs. Carradine tensed himself. Death, when it came, was swift and sudden and unexpected. There was a twin flash of quicksilver in the pale moonlight. The two guards jerked as though struck by invisible fists. Swaying, they put up their hands towards their throats where the hafts of the knives protruded from the exposed flesh. Then they went down on their knees, almost in unison, toppling onto their faces without a moan.

Now for the dogs, thought Carradine tensely. Get those dammed dogs! Now that the long chains had been released from the dead fingers of the guards, the hounds leapt forward, sprinting across the open stretch of ground, ears lying back on their heads, teeth showing white in the gaping jaws.

Get them, his mind screamed. *They'll scent us within seconds and then it will all be over.* Even as the thought crossed his mind, the nearest of the three brutes suddenly swerved and came bounding directly towards him. Instinctively he cringed back and gripped the knife tightly in his fist, the blade thrust out, his legs twisted beneath him in the hope that he might get in a death thrust before those bared fangs sank into his throat.

From somewhere close at hand there came a faint hiss, a half-heard sound above the thumping of his heart and the pounding of the blood through his temples. Then the dog lurched sideways, clawing ineffectually at the air for a moment before collapsing onto its side. The claws scrabbled feebly for a second. Then it lay absolutely still.

Carradine looked away from the sprawling animal on the dirt. The other two dogs had been stretched out near at hand and the girl had caught his arm, half-dragging him towards the sheer wall at the back of the building. Hell, but that small solitary window seemed a long way up from the ground. The others came running in from all sides. Tai Fan stood against the wall, legs braced apart, his hands pressed hard against stone. Carradine saw then how they were going to reach the window.

Within moments, there was a human ladder against the wall. 'I will go up first,' said Ts'ai Luan. 'Then you must follow quickly. The window will not be locked.'

Before he could ask any further questions, the girl had shinned up the tower of men until she stood balanced on top, some five feet below the window. Damn, thought Carradine, what was he expected to do now? Tai Fan grunted hoarsely and jerked his head slightly. Drawing a deep breath into his lungs, Carradine took a tight grip on himself and began to climb, pulling himself up with his hands, trying to shut his mind to the strain these men must surely be under. Eventually he was standing on the shoulders of the topmost man, immediately behind Ts'ai Luan, holding on to her shoulders to steady himself.

'What now?' he asked through tightly clenched teeth.

'The window,' she said harshly. 'You must reach it. Hurry!'

'But how — ?'

'Climb onto my shoulders.' There was a note of urgency in her voice.

Carradine hesitated for only a fraction of a second. The girl bent her knees slightly, took his weight on her shoulders, then straightened up until his fingertips hooked around the ledge of the window. Carradine tried not to think of the human ladder beneath, concentrating all of his energies on opening the window. The breath was harsh and painful in his throat. By using all of his strength, he succeeded in levering it open and hauling himself inside, dropping lightly on the balls of his feet into the dim corridor. Reaching down, he caught the girl's wrists and pulled her inside. Seconds later, the rope which Tai Fan carried coiled about his middle came snaking up towards the window. On the second attempt he caught it and drew it in. There was an iron grille set in the far wall. Working swiftly, he looped the rope through it, knotted it firmly, then held on to it as the others came climbing up the sheer wall, the mountainous bulk of Tai Fan bringing up the rear.

6

The Female of the Species

The knife held loosely in his right hand, only dimly aware of the feel of cold metal against his fingers, Carradine padded softly and slowly, but not with the ultra-cautious movements of a man anticipating trouble — more with dream-like slowness, and the half-belief of having accomplished something he had never thought possible. Here they were, in the stronghold of the Red Dragon, and somewhere here was Chao Lin, the man he had come to find. The building was not silent. There was a strange subdued murmur of sound which seemed to come from all around them. Carradine recognised it as a blend of humming dynamos providing the lighting and heating, the muffled clatter of typewriters from the floor below, and other indefinable noises which went to make up the heartbeat of this dreadful place.

His train of thought was lost abruptly. Tai Fan took his arm, motioned with his head towards the far end of the corridor, then moved one finger across his throat in a universal gesture. There might be guards. If so, they would have to be killed silently. He nodded to indicate that he understood.

They started moving again, Carradine's face grim at the prospect of what lay ahead. Ten yards from the end of the corridor the girl paused and caught his arm. There came the sound of voices from somewhere around the corner. The clatter of booted heels on the stairs came a moment later. Long, dancing shadows thrown by the light behind the men appeared across the floor of the passage. Carradine closed his fingers around the hilt of the knife. There were three shadows, grotesquely elongated; first the bodies and then the long legs.

The men were talking loudly among themselves, totally oblivious to their danger. Carradine tensed. Out of the corner of his eye he saw the others ranged along one wall, pressing their bodies close to it, the

168

pale light glittering off the blades of the drawn daggers. The three men approached the top of the stairs. An instant later they appeared less than ten yards away. For a moment there was a taut, stunned silence as they stared at each other. Then Tai Fan drew back one huge arm, flicked it forward and one of the men died instantly with a knife in the jugular, a dark red stain pouring down his neck and into the collar of his tunic. Another man died a moment later as he made a futile attempt to unsling the rifle over his shoulder. The third man, a trifle more quick-witted than his companions, hurled himself to one side; the thrown knife missed his shoulder by less than an inch and clattered metallically against the wall behind him. As Carradine watched, fascinated, the Chinese suddenly hurled himself forward, the butt of the rifle lifted as he began the downward swing which would bring it crashing against the side of Carradine's head.

Everything had happened so quickly that only instinct saved him at that moment. Dropping to his knees, he dived for the man's legs. As he whirled sideways at the same time, he expected to feel the impact of the gun on his skull. But the move had taken the man completely by surprise. He stumbled. A knee thudded into the back of Carradine's neck as he scrambled onto one knee. He saw the other struggling to regain his balance, one hand thrust out against the wall in an effort to steady himself, the other still gripping the butt of the gun as he reversed it, fingers moving down the stock towards the trigger guard.

Carradine's muscles tightened. In a violent corkscrew of motion, he forced himself upward. His left shoulder caught the man under the leg and exerting all of his strength, he threw him completely off-balance. The long steel blade sliced into the guard's stomach with a sickening feel as if it was sliding into lard. He pushed with all of the force in his arm and shoulder until the knuckles felt the rough cloth of the uniform; then he twisted hard with his wrist. A thin bleat of sound came from the other's lips, the flailing arms seeking to catch him around the neck.

Drawing a harsh gasp of air into his heaving lungs, Carradine pulled himself upright and stared down into the terrible face that sank slowly to the floor, the lips drawn back from stained, broken teeth, the eyes wide and fixed with the life ebbing swiftly from them. Slowly, agonisingly, the dying man strove to lift the rifle, to bring it to bear on him, to press the trigger with the last ounce of strength left in him. Then the sweating face dropped back with a sharp, abrupt movement. The peaked cap fell off the shaven skull as the head struck the ground.

Carradine swayed and panted hoarsely through his clenched teeth. There was sweat on his forehead, trickling into his eyes, stinging them as he blinked several times. In the steady, ringing silence, he heard Ts'ai Luan say urgently: 'Are you all right, Steve?'

With an effort he nodded his head, struggling to clear it of the grey fog that swirled within his brain. Tai Fan moved purposefully forward, grasped two of the bodies by the high collars, lifted them clear of the ground as if they were little more than children, and hauled them back down the corridor to where Ts'ai Luan had moved away towards one of the doors. She opened it cautiously, peered inside, then nodded. Less than a minute later, all three bodies were out of sight and there was no sign in the passage that death had struck three times.

There was no one on the stairs as they made their way down to the second floor, and the long corridor, with the powerful lights set close to the ceiling, was also empty. Carradine gave it only a quick, cursory glance, then followed the others down towards the lower floors. The muted humming of machines from behind the closed doors reached their ears as they progressed towards the basement. This was going to be the most dangerous part of the job, he thought grimly. And they were working against time now. Sooner or later those two guards on the grounds were going to be missed and once their bodies were discovered, the fat would really be in the fire; the entire building would be searched, every entrance and exit sealed. There was the feel of inexorable time breathing down the back of his neck.

A few more seconds. A few more yards. Then they were at the bottom of the stairs. Ahead of them the long corridor, with soldiers on the other floors, stretched away into the distance. But here there was one big difference: there were no brilliant lights set against the ceiling. The passage was in almost total darkness, except for a few beams of light which slanted out from the doors on either side.

'Better than we had hoped,' murmured Ts'ai Luan. 'At least we have the advantage of darkness.'

Carradine paused, then nodded. There were likely to be several prisoners down here and there would be an inevitable delay until they discovered the cell which housed Chao Lin. But there was nothing to be done about that. Leaving Tai Fan at the end of the corridor, close to the bottom stairs to keep watch, they inched their way along the darkened passage. As they moved forward, Carradine noticed that at intervals there were long recesses set in the walls between certain of the doors. It was not until he was less than five feet from the nearest that it came to him why they were there. Yes, damn it! There was a small table set back into the wall and a man seated at it, a snub-nosed machine-gun resting beside his chair within easy reach of his right hand. Carradine straightened himself and touched the girl on the shoulder, nodding towards the recess, placing a finger to his lips.

Flattening his body against the wall, he inched along for a couple of feet and then warily edged his head around the corner. He took a single, all-embracing look and then drew back, waiting for the flooding of his heart to settle back to normal. The guard was half-asleep, his head nodding forward onto his arms, any thought of danger so far from his thoughts that he was completely relaxed.

Carradine stood quite still, tensing himself, measuring in his mind's eye the distance to the other. Then he thrust the knife back into his belt, grinned tightly at the girl as she looked at him in momentary surprise, and motioned her to stay where she was. Inching an eye around the corner again, he saw that the man had not changed his position. He still leaned forward in his chair, the back of the neck exposed in the faint light which filtered through a nearby door. Stiffening the fingers of his right hand, Carradine sucked in a gust of air, then took the three quick, silent steps which brought him immediately behind the unsuspecting man. The edge of his hand smashed against the nape of the proffered neck. Without a sound the other jerked forward. Before the man's face could hit the table, Carradine had swung the palm of his other hand beneath the chin, jerking it back. There was a faintly audible snap, then the Chinese slumped sideways in the chair. The eyes were open as if in stunned surprise, but they were rolled up so that only the whites showed and when he felt the flaccid wrist, there was no detectable pulse.

Ts'ai Luan moved swiftly past him, scarcely pausing to give the dead guard a second glance. She reached the closed door, stretched up on tiptoe and peered through the iron grille set in the stout wood. Turning, she shook her head, then moved quickly on to the next. Carefully Carradine bent, hooked his hands under the man's armpits, and drew him silently out of the chair, pulling him around the table where he laid him on the floor, out of sight of anyone walking along the corridor. It would not allay suspicion for long, but at the moment, seconds were precious and vital.

Ts'ai Luan uttered a faint sound as the breath gushed from her lips. He glanced up quickly. She motioned him forward.

'My uncle,' she said breathlessly. 'He is in there!'

'Then the guard must have the keys with him.' He went back to the inert body and rolled it over onto its back. There was a small bunch of keys attached to the man's belt. Swiftly he pulled them off and went back to the girl. The first three keys did not fit, but the fourth turned easily in the lock and he swung the door open, praying that no one further along the corridor would hear the sound or notice the faint beam of yellow light which spilled out into the passage.

The room was bare except for a table in

the middle and a low bunk against one wall. The man who lay on the bunk lifted his head weakly as they burst in. For a moment there was a look of loathing and resignation on the lined face, an expression which changed quickly to one of relief and stunned surprise.

'Ts'ai Luan!' The voice was a dry, husky whisper which scarcely carried across the room.

The girl said something urgently, in rapid Chinese that Carradine could not understand, and he saw the other nod. The old man's gaze flickered in his direction. In faultless English, he said softly: 'So you are the agent from London?' As Carradine nodded wordlessly, he went on: 'I knew they would send someone but I never thought to see you here, my friend.'

'There were times when I didn't expect to make it myself,' Carradine said dryly. 'But there is no time now to talk. That will come later. We have to get you out of here before the alarm is raised. There are enough dead men lying around to make that a certainty within the next few minutes.' Even as he spoke, he noticed the heavy chain around the man's ankle, a chain which was securely fastened to a shackle in the wall. One glance at the padlock near Chao Lin's ankle told Carradine, with a sinking feeling in his chest, that none of the keys he had taken from the dead guard would fit. What now? Desperately, he forced himself to think clearly. This was something they had not foreseen.

There was no time to hang about. Any moment now and one of the guards would be missed. Were they going to be foiled at the very last minute after coming so far?

Again it was a girl whose quick-witted mind supplied the answer. She turned quickly on her heel and moved like a wraith into the passage. Less than ten seconds later she was back, with Tai Fan close on her heels. The huge Chinese took one swift look at the chain, then grasped it in both hands close to the point where it encircled the other's ankle. Slowly, inexorably, the other began to pull. Sweat showed in tiny beads on his face and the great muscles under the tunic bulged as he exerted tremendous pressure. God, but the man was terrifically strong. Incredibly, the metal began to bend. Then, with an explosive snap, one of the links burst.

Dropping the length of chain onto the bare mattress, Tai Fan bent, caught Chao Lin around the waist and hoisted him over his shoulders, taking the other's weight without any effort.

Now to get out of this fearful place! As they made their way silently up the steep stairs to the third floor the building continued to hum and throb all about them. It seemed incredible, he thought to himself, that less than seven minutes had passed since he had swung in through that window. Yet even in that short space of time someone could have discovered that rope in the corridor, and there could be a party of guards waiting for them.

But miraculously, the corridor, when they finally reached it, was empty. The rope was where they had left it, snaking down through the half-open window. Swiftly, without speaking, the men climbed over the ledge and were gone from sight. Carradine waited while Tai Fan, still carrying Chao

Lin with one hand clasped tightly around the other's middle, lowered himself to the ground, then followed, ignoring the burns on the palms of his hands as he slid down. He held the end of the rope while Ts'ai Luan descended, then they were running over the open ground, into the deserted street and across to where the truck waited in the mouth of the narrow alley.

Still no sound came from the building a hundred yards away; nothing to indicate that there was any pursuit. But their luck would only hold for so long, Carradine thought grimly. It would not be long before all hell erupted. Carefully, Tai Fan placed Chao Lin in the back of the vehicle. The girl climbed in and as Carradine ran around to the front and slid into the seat, Tai Fan squeezed his huge bulk beneath the wheel. There was a broad smile on his moon-face. *He's actually enjoying this,* thought Carradine. God, he must hate the Communists. Sooner or later there would be a price on this man's head once the finger of suspicion was pointed at him. Not that Tai Fan would mind overmuch. In many countries there were men like him — men who lived and died by violence, fighting for lost causes. Outwardly a gentle giant, he killed viciously and expertly without asking questions, without a qualm on his conscience, whenever the situation dictated.

Tai Fan switched on the ignition. In the stillness, the noise seemed deafening. God, but that would be heard for miles. The engine started, then died. Unhurriedly, Tai Fan tried again. This time it fired. He let in the clutch, took the brake off, and they moved slowly out into the main street. Spinning the wheel, the other guided the truck past the lighted building, heading out of the city. For a moment, Carradine was on the point of telling the other they were going the wrong way, then he sat back. The other's reason was obvious when he paused to think about it. If there should be any pursuit, they could easily be stopped by roadblocks in the city. A radio warning from the Red Dragon Headquarters and every patrol in Canton would be alerted and on the lookout for them. Out in the darkness of the countryside, they would have a far better chance of throwing off any pursuers.

Very soon, the lights of Canton were left behind and Tai Fan switched on the powerful headlights as they drove through the absolute darkness along a winding, twisting road which, from Carradine's scanty knowledge of the area, led westward towards the hills. Settling back in the seat, he fought his taut muscles, forcing them to relax. So far, so good. But the Red Dragon would not give up easily. Once it was discovered that Chao Lin was gone, a full-scale hunt would be mounted for them.

Tai Fan was pushing the truck to its utmost limit, skidding around corners which showed abruptly in the probing beams of the headlights scant seconds before they came upon them. He seemed to know the road intimately and after a few scares, Carradine was content to sit back and allow the other to drive as he thought fit, suddenly confident in the other's ability to get them safely to wherever they were headed.

Even now, it was almost impossible to

believe that they had got away with it without a scratch. The enemy had been so supremely confident that their Headquarters was impregnable that the thought of anyone breaking in and rescuing one of the prisoners did not seem to have ever occurred to them, beyond the normal precaution of doubling the guard.

They kept up a good speed along the winding road, the heavy truck bouncing and jolting precariously from side to side. It was necessary that they should put as much distance between themselves and Canton as possible. Through the window, he had a blurred impression of low hedges, an occasional hut, which flashed by in a haze of shadows. The moon threw very little light over the scene and they passed no traffic on the road.

They drove through a small village. Not a single light showed in any of the houses on either side. For all the signs of life there were, it might have been a ghost town, abandoned decades before. Half a mile further on, the road branched. Tai Fan took the right-hand branch. Slowly, they began to climb. The note of the engine changed subtly, straining a little as the gradient increased.

The headlight beams bobbed and swayed as they bumped over the uneven road surface. Evidently the Chinese Communists were not concerned with keeping the roads in good repair unless they were important ones, linking the military sites with the big cities. He wondered vaguely where this particular one went. Most likely it climbed the hills and then meandered into the plains on the other side.

His thoughts gelled abruptly in his head. A brief flash of light showed for a fraction of a second in the wing mirror on the side of the truck. Wrenching his head around, he watched the flat, smooth glass. For a long moment there was nothing visible. Had he imagined it? In the darkness, with his thoughts in such turmoil, it was easy to be tricked.

Then it came again. For the first time, he saw it clearly. The unmistakable twin glow of headlights far back down the road. God, it hadn't taken them long to get after them! The others were perhaps two miles away, approaching the village they had just passed through. Would their pursuers guess which of the two roads they had taken? Would the red tail lights, small as they were, give them away? Keeping a close watch on the other vehicle, he fancied that it was moving more slowly now, as if the driver was trying to read their minds and outguess them. Then the headlights turned in their direction.

Now they were for it! It was impossible to tell the kind of vehicle that was behind them, but without doubt it would not be as heavy and unwieldy as the truck and it was only a matter of time — a very short time — before they caught up with them. He touched Tai Fan's arm, motioned to the mirror, and saw the other nod in understanding. The truck lurched forward as the driver pressed his foot down on the accelerator.

Reaching forward in the dimness, Carradine found the Luger where he had left it, checked it carefully, then held it on his knee. If the worst came to the worst, he was prepared to sell his life dearly.

Out of the edge of his vision, he

glanced at Tai Fan. The big man did not seem unduly worried at the prospect of being followed, even though he must surely have realised who it was on their tail.

They swung sharply around a right-angled bend, still climbing. Through the window, Carradine caught a brief glimpse of needle-tipped rocks which thrust up on the edge of a deep precipice. Hell, they had only to side-swipe a couple of yards and they were over the side and God alone know how deep that sheer drop was. He swore under his breath. In the small mirror the headlight seemed nearer; they were clearly gaining on them with every passing minute. His fingers tightened convulsively on the butt of the Luger. If only the others in the back had guns, they may be able to stop and make a fight of it; might even up the odds a little. But they had nothing more potent or lethal than throwing knives. What sort of chance did they have? The answer to that was not one to give anyone a feeling of confidence.

Tai Fan was leaning forward in his seat

now, the brilliant headlights rising and falling hypnotically, picking out the edge of the narrow road, vanishing into nothingness whenever the light wavered over the edge of the drop.

Did the other have some kind of plan for throwing those men off their tail? he wondered, noticing once more that there was no worry on the big man's broad, fleshy features. If he had, then Carradine failed to see what it might be. This road could go on and on for miles before they reached another village and even then, the chances of them getting help against men of the dreaded Red Dragon organisation were slim indeed.

Abruptly, Tai Fan switched the head-lights on full. And it was now possible, in the clear air, to see for more than two hundred yards. Carradine edged forward, peering through the windscreen. There was something up ahead of them, in-distinguishable at first, but with details becoming clearer as they thundered towards it. Then he saw that it was a narrow, humped-backed bridge, one which prob-ably spanned a small, swift-running stream which raced down the side of the hill and plunged in a miniature waterfall off the edge. On one side there was a sheer wall of rock, on the other a low stone bridge which, as they came close to it, showed signs of extensive repairs. Carradine could visualise why these repairs would be needed. In the dark, especially in rain or snow, this road would become treacherous in the extreme. God alone knew how many poor devils had failed to take the road at that point and gone crashing to their deaths many hundreds of feet below.

Tai Fan held the wheel easily in his massive hands, guiding the truck through with the dexterity of long experience. Less than twenty yards further on, a dark cleft showed in the rock face to their right. With a bleat of protesting rubber, the other jammed his foot hard on the brakes. There was a terrifying moment when it seemed that the ungainly truck would spin completely out of control and join the others which had gone over the lip of the precipice. Then the wheels gripped and they came to a bone-jarring halt. Pushing the gear lever into reverse, he backed into the cleft. Stones and pieces of rock grated beneath the truck. In the same second, the other switched off the lights.

For a moment, Carradine could see nothing in the pitch blackness which clamped tightly about them now that the lights had been extinguished. Just what did the other intend to do? Hope that their pursuers would pass them by without noticing they were there? Even if they did, it would only be a temporary respite. Those men would not be fooled for long. They would soon realise what had happened and come back looking for them.

Revving up the engine, Tai Fan drove onto the road, edging the truck towards the looming shadow of the bridge, guiding the vehicle more by feel than sight.

Now Carradine could just see the probing headlights of the oncoming car. Judging from the size, it appeared to be some kind of army vehicle. Obviously the Red Dragon would not take chances; they would have guessed that some organisation had been necessary to rescue Chao

Lin and would have sent sufficient means to deal with them. They were now less than fifty yards from the side of the bridge, but at the moment, because of the hump on the road, only the upthrusting beams of the headlights were visible, spearing up into the dark star-strewn heavens.

A split second before it happened, Carradine realised what Tai Fan was waiting for. He felt a sudden leap of his heart. God, why hadn't he realised it before? Of course!

The other's hand reached out and flicked the switch of the powerful lights. The brilliant, eye-searing beams leapt out over the top of the bridge. The other driver had no chance at all. No one could possibly have looked into those twin beams from that distance and not be totally blinded. For perhaps ten seconds, the army vehicle continued on its original course, heading over the bridge. Vaguely, Carradine had a glimpse of a strained face peering through the windscreen; of a hand going up across the eyes in an effort to shut out the blinding glare. Then the army driver swerved instinctively. He must have stamped on the brake at the same moment, for the wheel seemed to suddenly lock. But the other was seconds too late. Screeching wildly, the small truck careened towards a low parapet of the bridge and struck the corner of the wall with a rending crash and a tearing of metal. One front wheel tilted upward under the shattering impact. The truck teetered on the edge of the ravine as though reluctant to begin the downward plunge to total destruction. Then the nose tipped as the stone parapet gave way. Slowly, like some old movie in slow motion, the truck slid over the edge of the precipice with a grinding of metal on stone.

The first resounding crash came a couple of seconds after it had disappeared; then another, more distant. Carradine could see nothing of it as it hurtled downward to the bottom, but it was not difficult to see it in his mind's eye, twisting and turn ing over and over as it fell, striking against the rocky outcrops. As he thrust open the door and climbed out into the cold night air, there came the sound of the final crash far down on the rocks; then a sudden spark, a flash and a boiling gout of flame and smoke which lifted high from the bed of the gorge. No one could possibly have survived that fall, he thought, his breath hissing through his teeth.

There was a soft movement at his back. The girl had climbed from the rear of the truck and come towards him, holding on to his arm as he peered down. Her face bore no trace of expression and her dark eyes were inscrutable.

'At least it must have been quick,' Carradine said harshly. 'That driver never had a chance once those lights blinded him.'

'Put it out of your mind, Steve,' she said quietly. 'They would have done exactly the same to us if the positions had been reversed and not given it a further thought.'

Slowly, Carradine made his way back to the truck. Behind the wheel, Tai Fan was smiling broadly, evidently pleased with his handiwork. Carradine gave a quick nod as the other held up his right hand.

'You did all right, Tai Fan,' he said grimly. 'I'm more glad than ever that you're not on the other side.'

'Tai Fan fought with the Nationalist

Army against the Japanese,' Ts'ai Luan told him. 'He hates anything the Communist regime stands for.'

'I can understand that.'

'No doubt you are wondering where we are going, and why we came this way,' the girl said. 'There is a place in the hills where we can hide in safety. You will want to talk with my uncle as soon as possible. In Canton, it would have been dangerous. That is why we chose to come up here. Those fools will never find us.' There was a note of contempt in her soft voice.

'How is Chao Lin?' he asked. They stood by the side of the narrow road while Tai Fan edged the truck in reverse to the narrow opening in the rock, turning the vehicle. Now that the danger was past for the time being, they could afford to take their time.

'He has been tortured, but he never talked.' For the first time, a note of pride entered her voice and she drew herself up as she looked at him. 'He will need medical attention as soon as we can get it for him. But by dawn he will be able to talk to you. He is sleeping now, completely exhausted.'

'Good. It is quite obvious from what has already happened, that whatever information he has locked away inside here — ' He tapped his forehead significantly. ' — it is of the utmost importance.'

One of the men called to them from the back of the truck. There was no time for more talk. It was possible that those men who had just gone to their deaths over the side of the ravine had not been alone; that there may be others following some distance behind. If this was indeed the case, then that petrol fire at the bottom of the valley could be a direct giveaway. As a beacon, it would be visible for miles in almost every direction.

They went back to the truck. Carradine helped the girl on board, then walked around to the front and slid into the seat beside Tai Fan. Two minutes later they were driving quickly towards the ridged summit of the hills with the three-quarter moon just reaching its zenith and beginning its long slide down towards the western horizon.

7

The Desperate Hours

For part of the night, in spite of the
bouncing, swaying motion of the truck,
Carradine managed to sleep. When he
woke, his body stiff and sore, there was
grey dawn around them and they were
high in the hills, with gaunt bare rock on
every side. Tai Fan still sat as imperturb-
able as ever behind the wheel, looking as
fresh as when they had started out. Did
that man ever need to sleep? Carradine
recalled the way in which he had held that
ladder of men beneath the window at the
rear of the Red Dragon Headquarters and
knew that Tai Fan was a little more than
an ordinary man.

Straightening up, he stifled a yawn. In
the pale grey light, he saw that the road
had narrowed now and was little more
than a track through the rocks. At some
time during the early hours of the

morning they must have swung around the summit of the hill and cut back on themselves, for they appeared to be heading north-east again in the direction of the rosy flush which marked the dawn.

Stretching his legs as far as he could in an effort to ease the cramp which lanced through his muscles, Carradine sat up in his hard seat. Tai Fan momentarily turned his head, then lifted the fingers of his left hand before pointing through the wind-screen along the twisting road ahead. What did that mean? Five more minutes — or five hours? He forced a grim nod. He was not sure that he could stand another five hours of this.

Spinning the wheel, Tai Fan sent the truck hurtling toward seeming destruc-tion over the edge of the track, then straightened it up with an almost contemptuous flick of a huge wrist. A few moments later, they topped a low rise and against the grey and red brightness of the swiftly approaching dawn, Carradine saw that less than half a mile ahead of them the ground levelled out into some kind of plateau. Backing it up was a sweep of rock with some kind of cave set into it, although in the deep shadow thrown by the dawn it was difficult to make out details. Tai Fan touched his arm, jerked a thumb towards the plateau and smiled happily. Five minutes it had been!

Tai Fan drove the truck straight into the mouth of the cave. There was a wide overhang which would prevent them from being spotted from the air, if the Chinese considered that Chao Lin was sufficiently important a person to use planes to search for him. The sun came up, literally bounding from below the horizon, flooding the hills with light. In the clear, sparkling air, it was possible to see for miles over the vast panorama which lay spread out beneath them. Now that they were there, it seemed a reasonably attractive place, Carradine thought. Plenty of shelter for, the cave went far back into the hillside, and he had noticed that there were narrow passages running off to the rear. There were, too, he had seen, large wooden boxes and crates which he guessed contained stores and food. Enough to feed an army, he reckoned. Not only that, but it would be possible

197

for a handful of men to hold off an army here. The track petered out at the mouth of the cave and there was only one approach — the way they had come. Even from the air it would be virtually impregnable.

'This was one of the last strongholds of the Nationalist forces when they fought the Communists,' said Ts'ai Luan. 'As a fortress, it is ideal.'

'And how long have you known of it?'

She shrugged. 'For many years now. The Communists suspect that there is a place in the hills, but they have never found it. Even if they did, they would find it extremely difficult to capture.' Her eyes sparkled and there was a look of extreme vitality on her face which he had found so attractive and fascinating. Once more, he regretted that they should have been forced to meet under such strained circumstances.

Inside the wide opening, he could see the rest of the men hard at work. The girl was watching his face with a look of concern and tenderness. She smiled up at him and took his arm in hers. What was going on behind those dark eyes? he wondered. Now they were veiled a little as though in thought.

'Before you speak to my uncle, there is something I have to show you,' she said softly. 'It won't take long.'

'All right.' He allowed her to lead him across the rock-strewn plateau, to a spot about fifty yards from the cave entrance. Now they were out of sight of the others; it was almost as though they were the only two people still alive in the world.

'Here,' said the girl. Her voice was suddenly solemn and there was a change to the quality of her movements as she bent and held back a straggling bush which somehow succeeded in draining some little nutrition from the thin soil.

Carradine glanced over her shoulder. There was the glint of metal among the rocks with a couple of cotton-covered wires leading off into the boulders in the direction of the cave. 'What is it?' he asked, curious.

'The top of a landmine,' said Ts'ai Luan, her voice flat. 'This is one of twelve sited in and around the cave. They are all linked to a central point. If the enemy should find us, then our last act will be to detonate them. They will find nothing, those who are still alive. I understand that the mines are powerful enough to destroy everything.'

Carradine straightened abruptly. 'I see.' God, he thought, how inane a couple of words could be!

'It has to be this way,' she went on calmly. 'We all know far too much. It is better that we should die in a split second than that they should take us alive, back to that place in Canton. We all know what that would mean.'

Carradine felt suddenly tight and cold. There did not seem to be anything he could say. Ts'ai Luan stood quite still for a moment and then reached out her hands, took a tight hold on his lapels, and tugged hard at them. With an effort, he forced his mind away from the thoughts that raced through it. Leaning forward, he placed his arms around the slender waist, pulled her almost roughly to him and kissed her hard upon the lips. She did not resist, but clung to him tightly, as though afraid to let him go.

'My God, Ts'ai Luan,' he said thickly. 'This is one hell of a way to meet each other. We might just as well meet in the middle of a full-scale shooting war.'

'Hush, Steve,' she said. She placed a finger softly on his lips. 'I knew there could be very little between us when we first met. But time means nothing. A day comes and a day goes. Tomorrow will become today, and then there will be more tomorrows, but none of us know how many there will be for each of us. Soon, if you are successful, you will go away and leave me. I know that. But it does not trouble me. So why let it trouble you? We have a little time together.'

She kissed him again. Now there was a fierceness, a passion in her which matched his own feelings. Almost brusquely, he pushed her away from him. For a moment there was a look in her eyes of some small animal being punished for something it did not understand. Then she smiled up at him. 'I understand, Steve. There is work to be done. You must question my uncle.'

He nodded wordlessly and forced his mind away from her. As they made their way slowly towards the cave, he tried not to think of those twelve cylinders of metal sited strategically around them, with the detonator wires all leading to the one spot. Hell, what a situation to be in, he thought fiercely. A place of comparative safety and yet with sleeping death lying all about them.

Chao Lin was lying on a pile of blankets in the far corner of the cave, away from the track, when he entered. As he squatted beside the other, he saw the long, fresh scars on the man's lined features and the bandages around the fingers resting in front of him. Chao Lin followed the direction of his eyes and said in a low voice: 'Our friends can be extremely persuasive at times, especially when they are anxious to learn something.'

'The bamboo treatment?' asked Carradine softly.

Chao Lin nodded, lifted his hands weakly and stared at them, at fingers which were swollen not merely by the bandages taped around them. Carradine felt a little shudder go through him at the thought of what this man must have suffered before they had succeeded in getting him away. Most likely a refinement of the Japanese torture treatment, thrusting long thorns and splinters of bamboo beneath the nails to make their victims talk. There would have been other things too about which he knew little.

'I'm sorry,' he said simply.

'But why be sorry? We all know the risks we are taking when we work for freedom and liberation. I am not the first to have to suffer, nor will I be the last. It is not good that this should be so,' he added philosophically. 'But we must all accept life as we find it and try to change it for the better in any way we can. Only out of suffering does true victory come.'

'Confucius?' asked Carradine, forcing a tight smile.

The other shook his head slowly. 'The unworthy Chao Lin,' he answered. Then his tone sobered and his voice gained strength. 'But there is much to talk about and little time. You know, of course, about Kellaway, my Number Two in Hong Kong?'

'I know that he has a secret transmitter in his room and that he is probably in touch with Red Dragon agents inside Hong Kong, perhaps here in China.'

Chao Lin inclined his head slightly. 'That is so. I began to suspect him a little time ago. There were two cases to my knowledge when the enemy knew things which only he and I knew. And there have been too many little incidents which, taken together, would be stretching coincidence too far. There had to be a traitor somewhere and it was only logical to suspect him. But I had no proof. I knew that if anything happened to me, that if London did send someone out to check, he would automatically trust Kellaway and he'd be in deadly danger.'

'So you warned Ts'ai Luan about him — warned her to be on the lookout for me.'

'Yes.' The other lifted his head slowly and looked up at the girl standing nearby. 'She has proved extremely useful in the past, being able to get in and out of China with little difficulty and without arousing suspicion.' There was a faint gleam in the tired old eyes. 'There are still many people in China who wish to see the end of this present regime. As yet, they are not strong enough. But there will soon come a time when they will have their opportunity.'

'But what of this secret information you have?' prompted Carradine.

The other's face changed. 'That is a different matter, my friend. I tried to get the news through to London, but as you know, I was unfortunately prevented from doing so.'

'But I'm here now. With luck, I may be able to get it back if it's sufficiently important.'

'It is of the gravest importance. But it is now too late to send word to London. Before they could do anything about it, the test would have been carried out.'

'What sort of test? A new weapon?' Carradine thought of the first thing which came to his mind. 'A hydrogen bomb test, perhaps?'

'No, not that. We know they are working frantically to develop such a nuclear device. This is something different. Three months ago, one of my contacts sent word that a small but highly secret laboratory had been built near Lungmoonyunhsien about seventy miles north-east of Canton. He had managed to get himself in one of the working parties building the road from the town, and from what he saw and was able to describe to me it was clear that, although this was not an atomic installation, it was highly guarded and the site for top-secret work on some military weapon.'

Carradine recalled that it was Chao Lin who had supplied most of the initial information on the secret site in Sinkiang province which had led to the West discovering about the first Chinese atomic tests, and he gave an involuntary shudder as he wondered what more this man had found out.

Chao Lin continued: 'There are men in high places inside China who are not entirely in sympathy with the Communist regime — men who are extremely useful to me. Slowly the reports began to come in, but the picture they built for me was difficult to understand. Gradually, however, the picture clarified. There was news of precision ground optical parts being shipped there from all over China and one of their top scientists, Kao Fi Min, was put in charge of the work.'

Carradine narrowed his eyes. 'I've heard of him from somewhere,' he said tightly. 'Did he not deliver a paper in Moscow two years ago on recent developments in lasers?'

'That is the same man,' affirmed the other gravely. 'When I knew his name, I spent much of my time in Hong Kong reading what I could about these instruments, trying to discover some way in which they could be used as military weapons. The libraries there are quite up-to-date. It was not long before I began to see some of the possibilities myself. But even I had no idea how far these men had progressed. We thought they were concentrating all of their efforts on attempting to close the gap in the atomic race. Instead, part of their effort has evidently been directed in other fields. And believe me — ' He leaned towards Carradine, one hand on his wrist. ' — they are far ahead of Western scientists in this particular branch of science if my informant is correct. As I understand them, lasers are instruments which deliver pulses of light that are coherent in that they are all of the same frequency. From what I have read, lasers are quite capable of burning a hole through a steel plate within seconds, and the beam which they project is virtually completely parallel. There was one report I read which originated in America — and therefore I cannot vouch entirely for its accuracy — that it has been found possible to project a beam from a giant laser to the dark side of the moon, and that with a sufficiently large telescope it would have been possible to see the reflection of the light, a distance of a quarter of a million miles.'

'That may have been so, but — '

'Patience,' murmured the other. He raised himself from the blankets with an effort. 'There is more. Kao Fi Min has been working for two years in an attempt to perfect this terrible weapon of destruction. It is due to be tested for the first time at full power tomorrow. If it is successful, and the indications are that it

will be, then they will have in their hands
an offensive weapon of terrible potency.
You understand the full implications
behind this, my friend?'

'I do indeed.' Although Carradine's
knowledge of lasers and such things was
severely limited, he knew a little about
them. But something that could literally
smash a hole in an inch-thick sheet of
high-tensile steel within seconds . . . What
havoc could be wrought if the power were
stepped up sufficiently; and what of the
devilish refinements that had been added?
The Chinese were the first to use
gunpowder, although they hadn't utilised
it for warfare, leaving that to the West.
Their talents were doubtless undimin-
ished through the centuries but there was
no doubt that their attitudes and
ideologies had changed.

Chao Lin seemed to sense something
of Carradine's thoughts. 'You see now
why I said there was no time to warn
London and hope that they might be able
to do something. In twelve hours that
weapon will be tested. Unfortunately I
have no idea what the target will be, but

as you may know, since the Russians withdrew their anti-aircraft rockets from China, the Americans have been able to fly over the territory with impunity, photographing and recording all that has been taking place. Naturally, the Communist leaders do not like this, although they know that it has been happening. There are also American spy satellites operating over this country. I suppose it would not be amiss to believe that they have predicted the time of passage of one of these satellites and intend to use it as the target.'

Of course! It all began to fit, all of the little isolated bits of evidence slotting together into a recognisable pattern. No wonder the Red Dragon organisation wanted to be sure that Chao Lin did not talk. They could not be sure just how much he did know, or what he had discovered; yet no matter how little it was, he had to be stopped from passing news of this juicy little titbit to the West. Unlike the Chinese nuclear test, this must surely have been one of their best-kept secrets. He had certainly heard nothing whatever about it during his conversations with the Chief and he knew that if the other had even the slightest inkling, he would have said so before sending him on this assignment. The first the Western powers would know of this would be the sudden and unexpected loss of one of their satellites. Only then would they awaken to the unpleasant fact that China was not only a force to be reckoned with in terms of manpower, but also the leader in the art of destruction.

Carradine's face was suddenly tight and pale. *Twelve hours! Twelve hours in which to try to change the destiny of the world!* He clenched his hands in futility and despair.

★ ★ ★

The time must be about three o'clock, Carradine reflected, glancing up at the sun, already past its zenith and beginning the long slide down the western half of the sky. He pressed himself flat against the roof of the truck, the powerful binoculars against his eyes, staring into the harsh glare of the sunlight. Swiftly he adjusted the focusing ring. Details sprang into blinding clarity. Slowly he began to sweep the horizon from left to right. Ahead of him, the wide plain stretched as far as it was possible to see, clear to the sun-hazed horizon. Beyond it lay the South China Sea, with the safety of Hong Kong somewhere in that general direction. How far away it all seemed now. With an effort he thrust the idea from his mind and concentrated all of his senses into his eyes, alert for any movement, especially where the road led straight across his line of vision, linking the small town of Lungmoonyunhsien with the small cluster of buildings over to his right, the sunlight glinting on a multitude of glass windows. Half an hour before, there had been traffic on that modern stretch of road, but now it appeared deserted.

Even as he absorbed the topography of the valley, eyes probing and searching every dip and hollow for a possible source of danger, his mind was racing back over the events of that morning. After all of the good luck they had had the previous night when they had broken into the Headquarters of the Red Dragon in Canton and rescued Chao Lin from under their very noses; after they had, in the face of all the odds, succeeded in throwing off pursuit, it would have been only natural that their luck should change. But fortune had continued to smile on them. Not that it had been easy formulating any plan which had in it the smallest kernel of success. One thing had been blatantly obvious: If anything was to be done, they would have to do it. There was no one else in a position to smash this secret weapon and laboratory which had spawned it. Chao Lin had been certain that the plans for the instrument were still at the laboratory, and would remain there until after the test had been carried out and proclaimed a success. Then, perhaps, they would be taken to Peking where they would be put to the people as another example of the greatness of Mao Tse Tung.

They had left Chao Lin with one of the men and the other girl in the troupe — Ts'ai Luan had insisted on coming with them although her uncle had tried to persuade her to remain behind — and with the indomitable Tai Fan driving, they had made good time along the hill tracks before reaching the spot less than three miles from Lungmoonyunhsien. The journey had been uneventful. They had passed small groups of peasants by the side of the road shortly before midday and once a line of army vehicles heading in the opposite direction had approached, the leading driver beeping hard on his horn. Tai Fan had obediently pulled well over to one side to allow them to pass, but there had been no interference.

Lowering the binoculars produced for him from the stores kept in the cave, Carradine let them dangle around his neck, rubbing his eyes with his knuckles. He had expected the whole of southern China to be overrun with soldiers looking for them, yet there had been nothing like that. Was there a trap being built up against them somehow, somewhere; something of which they knew nothing as yet? It seemed distinctly possible, knowing the kind of men they were up against. General Lung Chan was not the kind of man to run the risk of losing his reputation — or his head — over the loss of his most important prisoner, without making every possible effort to recapture him and those responsible for freeing him.

Wriggling to the edge of the track, Carradine dropped down onto the road. Ts'ai Luan glanced up at him.

'There seems to be very little traffic on the road just now,' he said harshly. 'I wonder if there is any significance in that?'

The girl looked up at the sun for a moment, slitting her eyes against the light. 'They will almost certainly be working around the clock to get everything ready.'

'And we have to get inside somehow before we can do anything. That laboratory will be more closely guarded than any other place in China. It's out of the question that we could break in as we did with that other place in Canton.'

'There is only one way to get inside,' Ts'ai Luan said.

'And what is that?'

'While you were up there spying out the land, I have been thinking,' she said

215

indirectly. 'I was thinking that if this test they intend to carry out is so important, then some top-ranking military men will be there to see it.'

'Yes,' agreed Carradine thoughtfully. 'That's almost certain.'

'And they will certainly not come by the road we did. They will use the main road from Lungmoonyunhsien. So all we have to do is stop one of the staff cars and take their uniforms. It is as simple as that.'

Carradine looked at her in silence for long seconds without speaking, then gave a brief nod. 'It's not as simple as that, Ts'ai Luan,' he said softly. 'But it's the only way.'

★　★　★

The grip on Carradine's shoulder was tight and urgent. He turned his head sharply. The girl whispered fiercely: 'Something coming, Steve!'

Keeping his head well down, he thrust the lenses of the binoculars against his eyes. About a mile away, in the direction of the town, a small cloud of grey dust indicated the approach of some kind of vehicle. A staff car with some important officer inside, or a truck bringing up more reinforcements? If it was a truck, they would have to stay out of sight and let it go by. No point in throwing away everything trying to take on a score of soldiers. But if it was a staff car, then they would have to work fast.

Now the vehicle was only about half a mile away and coming up fast, and still the cloud of white dust thrown up by the wheels obscured most of it. Then, for a second, Carradine was able to see it clearly.

'It's a staff car,' he said sharply. 'Warn the others. They all know exactly what to do.'

The girl raised herself a little and waved her arm. There came a signal from the other side of the wide, concrete strip of the road. God, but this was going to take split-second timing, Carradine thought fiercely: hijacking a staff car in broad daylight on this open stretch of road. Yet they had committed themselves now. The prospect would have frightened him but for the sharp sense of excitement stirring within. This was what he had been trained for. This was his whole life since he had dedicated himself to the Service!

From the edge of his vision, he saw one of the men run out into the middle of the road, throwing himself down onto the concrete in the path of the oncoming car. Would the driver stop? Or would he simply drive on, over the inert body of what he considered to be simply a peasant, someone who was expendable? There was also the possibility that these men would be alert for danger.

He was answered at once. There came the squeal of brakes being applied. The speed of the car was checked. It made to swerve around the man lying in the road, then came to an abrupt stop less than ten yards away. Carradine saw the man beside the driver say something. Leaving the engine still running, the driver got out. There were two men seated on the back-seat of the car. Neither made any move as the driver advanced on the prone man.

Cradling the Luger in the crook of his

forearm, Carradine aimed it carefully. This was no time for niceties, no time to think of ethics of war, even in this sort of hole-in-the-corner fight. The driver, standing over the man on the ground, the toe of his boot thrust out to turn him over, suddenly jerked back as though struck in the chest. He seemed to develop a third eye in the centre of his forehead. Before the sharp echoes of the single shot had died away, before the body of the driver crashed to the ground, three things had happened simultaneously.

The girl, running like a gazelle, had reached the side of the car. The long-bladed knife in her hand was thrust against the short, squat man's neck, the tip of the blade pressing against the base of his throat. Tai Fan and two other men were at the back of the car, pulling open the doors, dragging the two officers out into the road, and Carradine had grabbed the dead driver by the collar and was dragging him out of sight into the brush by the side of the road.

By the time he got back to the car, the other three men were dead. Carradine did not like the idea of killing in cold blood any more than the next man, but they could not afford to risk any of these men getting free and raising the alarm. There was far too much at stake.

Less than three minutes passed before Carradine was seated in the back of the car, dressed in the uniform of one of the dead officers. Now his only regret was that none of the uniforms had been large enough to fit Tai Fan's mountainous bulk. The other would have been invaluable in the work they would have to do. The one consolation was that one of the other men, Tao Chia-Tu, having fought with the Nationalists during the long retreat across China shortly after the war, was an expert in demolition and sabotage.

Hoping that there would not be some kind of password to get into the top-secret laboratory, Carradine sat back as they drove along the dusty stretch of concrete road towards a low cluster of buildings in the distance. Barbed wire had been stretched around the site and he noticed that there were guard posts every couple of hundred yards with what looked like machine-gun nests and searchlights surrounding the place.

Unhesitatingly, they drove up to the front gate. The two guards on either side had snub-nosed automatic weapons over their shoulders. Would they recognise the car and wave it through — or would they stop it and demand to see papers? He held his breath until it hurt in his lungs. The man behind the wheel, his face expressionless, slowed a little as they approached; to have accelerated would have been fatal.

One of the guards stepped forward and raised his hand for them to stop. He came forward, one hand held through the strap of the gun. Stiffening in reflexive antici-pation, Carradine gripped the butt of the Luger, hidden from sight by the seat in front of him, his finger tight on the trig-ger. Maybe if there was trouble he could shoot both of the guards, giving the driver the chance to turn the car and head back before the alarm could be raised.

The guard bent, thrust his head through the open window beside the driver, allowed his gaze to slide over the four of them, then said something rapidly. The driver nodded, said something back, then let in the clutch as the guard straightened and stepped back a couple of paces. The next moment they were driving through the gate between the rows of barbed wire. The sense of relief was almost overwhelming. Evidently the other had been merely telling the driver where they were to park the car.

They pulled up beside several other cars and got out. Stretching his legs, Carradine forced himself to relax completely. So far, so good. But they were not out of the woods yet, not by a long way. He swept his glance around the site. The long, low building in front of which they had stopped was clearly a reception room with a small canteen to one side. Beyond it lay two L-shaped concrete-and-glass laboratories and off to one side, almost hidden by earthen mounds, was a perfectly flat piece of ground, built up by tons of dirt and rubble so that it was perhaps thirty feet above the rest of the site. In the centre of it, covered by some form of plastic sheeting, was a large ungainly shape at whose contours he could only guess. He felt a sudden quickening of his pulse. That must be the new weapon they intended to test!

A short, stocky man wearing a white coat came out of the reception building and walked towards them. He bowed slightly. 'I am Lao Ti,' he said deferentially. 'Personal assistant to Kao Fi Min, the Director of this project. If you will please come with me, I will take you to the others.'

★ ★ ★

It was the kind of conference room one would have expected to find in the American missile base at Cape Kennedy, rather than in this isolated, out-of-the-way place inside China, so mistakenly considered to be one of the more backward of the great powers when it came to scientific achievement. It was about thirty feet square with rows of deep chairs and a raised podium at one end, the walls and ceilings painted a pale, egg-shell blue and a thick carpet on the floor between the aisles.

As Carradine lowered himself into one

of the chairs, with Tao Chia-Tu beside him, he felt it difficult to suppress his natural surprise. If London ever got to hear about this, they would almost certainly revise their opinion of the Chinese. While Carradine took in the scene, Lao Ti came in, preceded by a tall, thin, bespectacled man in spotless white overalls. This, he felt sure, would be Kao Fi Min, the brains behind this project.

The latter proceeded to the chair behind the desk on the rostrum and sat down as Lao Ti stepped forward. The hubbub of conversation among the thirty or so of military officers in the room died down.

Lao Ti began quietly: 'I am extremely honoured to welcome you all to this laboratory so that you may witness one of the greatest advancements of Chinese science.' He inclined his head a fraction in the direction of the tall, thin figure seated in the chair nearby. 'You all know our revered Kao Fi Min, one of our foremost scientists and the designer of the instrument you're about to see. A weapon which will place China in the forefront of the world powers. A year ago, under pressure from the American imperialists, the Soviet Union withdrew its support of our scientific effort and also denied us further supplies of nuclear fuel. No doubt they considered that this would place us at a disadvantage as far as the development of weapons was concerned. However, what you are going to witness today will provide proof, if any were needed, that we do not have to rely on other nations for our own defence, or for our ability to further the cause of communism. We foresaw this change in Soviet policy and took the necessary steps to ensure that any effect would be only temporary. It is true that so far, we have only reached the stage of experimental detonations of atomic weapons and have not yet succeeded in constructing a hydrogen bomb to equal those of the Soviets and the Americans, but their leads are being narrowed rapidly. In the meantime, unknown to any other country, we have been quietly experimenting with other novel weapons. Kao Fi Min will now describe to you what we have achieved and the potentialities of this new weapon.'

Carradine switched his gaze as the skeletal figure rose to its feet and moved forward. For a moment, the mental image of Sax Rohmer's Doctor Fu Manchu flitted through his mind. The man must surely be just as that author had visualised him: the villain of the piece, the man who dreamed up mass destruction. Was that really fair? All over the world, and on the other side of the Iron Curtain too, there were men like Kao Fi Min working in highly secret laboratories, scheming up such terrible weapons, firmly believing that they were working to further the cause of democracy and freedom for the individual. Who was to say which side was in the wrong? When the bombs began to fall, they did so indiscriminately, destroying the innocent and the guilty alike.

He forced himself to concentrate on what the other was saying, hampered somewhat by his lack of fluency in the language. Fortunately the other spoke slowly and deliberately.

The first part of his speech was little more than a denunciation of the Russians, their former allies in this field. Listening

226

to him, Carradine was not sure just how fiercely the other really felt about the way in which they had been let down, or how much he had to say because it was expected of him — a phonograph record in his mind repeating over and over again a childish ritual which had to be observed because without it, one might be suspected of the wrong sorts of thoughts about the present regime.

Then the other came to the subject at hand. Carradine sat up more rigidly in his chair, wondering if something in what the other might say would give him a tiny clue as to how they might destroy this weapon and all that went with it. At the moment his mind was devoid of any possibilities. Little short of half a ton of high explosive would carry out the devastation needed to ensure that nothing remained of the weapon, or the site.

'The laser is simply an instrument for delivering a coherent beam of light in which all of the vibrations and the wavelengths reinforce themselves, so that there is no cancellation of energy. The beam projected is also one which is almost ideally parallel, there being no perceptible spread of energy even over long distances. From the beginning, it was realised that if only sufficient power could be fed into such a beam, it would provide a weapon of tremendous destructive energy. The prototype models were able to burn their way through sheet steel, but there still remained the problem of feeding sufficient energy into the system. This necessitated a fundamental change in the basic design of the laser. Once this had been carried out, there was a question of harnessing a source of energy powerful enough to provide us with all that we would require.' There was a pause. The other smiled thinly. 'Naturally, there is only one source of energy we could use. While the other world powers proudly proclaimed their success in harnessing nuclear energy for other than destructive uses, we went quietly ahead, building the first reactor in China beneath this laboratory. It had to be erected quickly. There was no way of telling how long it would be before someone else stumbled upon our secrets. However, it has now been functioning satisfactorily for more than seven months, providing us with light, heat and the source of energy for the weapon outside.'

For a long moment there was silence in the room. Carradine felt his skin begin to prickle and crawl uncomfortably. For a moment his thoughts went back to his last interview with the Chief in that office high above the busy London street. *'We believe that Chao Lin has stumbled upon some information concerning a secret weapon which the Chinese are developing. Your job will be to bring Chao Lin and details of this weapon out of China.'*

God, if the only way in which he could stop this thing was to destroy himself along with it, he knew he would have to do that. With all of the spy planes and satellites, and even with their monitoring stations placed strategically around China, their devices for picking up radioactive fallout and seismic receivers giving information about any explosions inside this country, the Americans would never guess at the magnitude of what faced them at this moment. For a second he wondered if the loss of one of their satellites might possibly provide them with a clue, then dismissed the thought even as it crossed his mind. Long before they ever got around to working out what could conceivably have happened, it would be far too late. Tensing himself, he gathered his reserves of strength and courage, focusing all of his thoughts into trying to think of some way of destroying this place completely and utterly.

Kao Fi Min continued: 'The computer we have has predicted the position of one of the American spy satellites we know to have been put into orbit so as to cross China every day. They do not know it, but this evening will be the last time it will pass over our country. By tomorrow, their scientists and technicians will be frantically striving to discover what could possibly have happened to destroy it. By then it will be too late. This weapon is only the prototype. With the knowledge we possess, it will be possible to construct even more powerful ones. Then no power on earth will be able to stop us.'

And he's right in every little detail, thought Carradine fiercely. Only a few more hours. God, was there no way to stop this? Even with Tao Chia Tu's undoubted abilities for sabotage, it was unlikely there would be enough high explosive on this site to make even the smallest impression, even if they had the opportunity of laying their hands on it. Yet they had to do something.

The faint murmur of conversation rose from all sides as Kao Fi Min finished speaking and sat down again. Carradine went meticulously over everything filed away in his brain. There had to be something! Then it came to him and he swore angrily at himself for not having realised it earlier. The nuclear reactor beneath the site. Hell, but there was enough power there to destroy not only these laboratories but everything for miles around. Carradine sat and thought, recalling everything he knew about these things. Somewhere there would be the nuclear cell itself in which the power was generated, possibly using uranium as fuel, with perhaps boron control rods to prevent the reaction from getting out of control. The only real difference between an atomic bomb and a nuclear reactor was the rate at which the energy was liberated. In the former case, the chain reaction built up to detonation point within microseconds; in the latter, because of the absorption of neutrons by the material of the control rods, it could not pass into the exposed stage but was liberated slowly and evenly.

The reaction could be speeded up or slowed down by the degree to which the control rods were inserted into the reaction medium. Now if they could be fully withdrawn, removed entirely, how long before the whole thing went up in a blaze of radiation, a boiling of that now-familiar and terrifying mushroom cloud?

He felt his stomach muscles quiver a little. Did it really matter? If there was sufficient time, then it was possible they might get out of the danger zone before everything went up. If not, then it was just too bad, but at least he would have succeeded. And if Chao Lin managed to get back to Hong Kong somehow, he could send on word to the Chief in London and their tiny squiggles on the seismographs throughout the Western world would be, in part, explained.

8

Holocaust!

The electric clock on the wall showed seven-fifteen. Outside, the sun was lowering swiftly towards the hills on the horizon to the west, throwing long shadows over the plain, purpling the distance with a deep haze. Some of the heat of the day was beginning to dissipate as a cooling wind blew from the north. It was approaching the end of another day and somewhere on the far side of the world, hurtling through the alternating darkness and light of space, the satellite continued on its endless circuit, the relays crackling as the cameras scanned the mottled surface below; cameras which would pierce cloud and haze and pick up details on the ground with an ease and clarity which almost passed belief.

On the artificial plateau to the east of the laboratories, the plastic covers had been removed from the gleaming metal and lenses of the weapon and now it lay ready, sleek and innocent-looking, the long cables running from it into the ground and down towards the long, quiet room far below.

There were three men inside the room, white-coated technicians whose job it was to watch the faintly flickering needles on the dials and gauges, to control the tremendous surge of power that passed through those armoured cables, thicker than a man's arm. One man sat at the desk in the centre of the room, a desk bare except for the small communicator at one end and the white telephone at the other.

Here, in spite of the sticky heat above ground, it was always pleasantly cool; in spite of the fact that less than twenty yards away, behind the tremendous shielding of lead and steel, nature in the raw was burning away at something approaching a million degrees centigrade, hotter than the surface of the Sun. If the men knew anything of this, they gave no sign. To the untrained eye, the scene would have been one of calm, unhurried efficiency, an air of everything being under complete control. Only these three men knew that everything was balanced on a razor-edge of uncertainty. So must those British and American scientists and military men have felt during the final preparations for the first test in the New Mexico desert. Now, after many years of research, the West had progressed to the stage where such nuclear power stations were almost completely automatic, with the latest safety devices built in so that there was virtually complete security. But this was not so here. The order to have this weapon ready had come down from Peking from the highest authority, and the development of the laser had not been equally matched by that which had gone into the building of this reactor. There had been phases in its construction when they had worked almost by guess-work and rule of thumb. Not that the military and the political leaders knew anything of this. As far as they were concerned, everything was functioning perfectly.

Outside, in the long, gleaming corridor,

two armed guards paced monotonously back and forth. Their presence there was purely a decorative one. The perimeter of the site was so well guarded that no one could possibly get inside and their duties consisted mainly of parading the corridor for six hours each day, then going off duty. Life was good for these men. Except for a day such as this one when a special show was needed to impress the high-ranking officers, discipline was noticeably lax. There was plenty of good food and rice wine to be had in the canteen and if a man got a little too drunk, no one paid much attention, certainly not the scientists who were running the place. They merely regarded the military as a necessary inconvenience and ignored their presence almost completely.

There was no one at the door on the left as Carradine and the others reached it. The doors were open; inviting. He gave a quick look up and down the corridor, then motioned them inside. It had been relatively easy to slip away from the rest of the crowd. The gleaming weapon on its concrete stand had been the centre of attraction and as far as he had been able to make out, they had been given the run of the place, with little if any restriction on their movements. No doubt if any of the senior scientists found them down in the reactor room, there may be some awkward questions to answer, but that was a risk they had to take. When the stakes were high, necessarily the risks were also.

Tao Chia-Tu glanced at the rows of buttons just inside the door and pressed one of them without hesitation. The doors whined shut with a faint sigh and a moment later they were going down. Carradine tried to estimate the distance. Presently the lift sighed to a stop. The door slid open. There was the faint hum of machinery all about them and he guessed that they were in the heart of the place. Excitement welled up inside him, contracting the muscles of his throat and lifting the small hairs on the nape of his neck. The doors had opened onto another corridor very similar to that above. Cautiously he stepped out, then tensed. There were two guards less than twenty feet away. Even as he stepped out of the lift, they both turned and stared at him in momentary surprise.

There was nothing for it now but bluff, to try to get the men off their guard. If he made the slightest move towards the Luger, it would be the last thing he did. Tao Chia-Tu moved past him. He said something loudly which Carradine didn't catch. For a moment the two guards remained suspicious, then they stiffened to attention. Carradine forced his wildly thumping heart into a slower, more normal beat. Act naturally, he told himself fiercely. The men would probably have been expecting someone to come down here. After all, what was more natural than someone in the ruling party wanting to see the source of the power being used for the weapon?

He walked right up to the door behind the two men, peered calmly through the glass panel, and nodded as if satisfied by what he saw.

Tao said harshly, a note of authority in his voice: 'This is the reactor room?'

It was evidently meant as a question and the guards nodded quickly.

'Then what is that man doing there?'

Tao pointed with his left hand. The two guards would have been less than human not to fall for it. Even as they were swinging round, leaning forward slowly to look over Carradine's shoulder into the control room beyond, a savage judo cut hit one of them behind the right ear. He pitched forward, head striking the wall with a sickening crunch. The second man opened his mouth to yell, fingers scrambling for the sling of his rifle. It was still halfway off his shoulder when Carradine hit him with all his strength across the adam's apple. With a gasping bleat, the other reeled backward, eyes rolling up in his head. Catching him beneath the arms, Carradine lowered the limp body to the floor.

'Get rid of them,' he said to one of the men. 'We'll take care of the men in here.'

Opening the door, he stepped inside, with Tao close on his heels. The three technicians looked round at this unexpected interruption, then the man at the table got to his feet and came forward. There was no suspicion on his face. He bowed slightly.

'We are indeed honoured that you should have considered coming here,' he said politely, impersonally. 'Perhaps there is something you wish to see?'

'We understand from what Kao Fi Min said this afternoon that this is the first nuclear reactor to be used for this purpose. They will be highly interested in our report of it in Peking.'

The mere mention of Peking was sufficient to make the other fawn even more than before. Carradine almost smiled at the way in which the three men hastened to show them everything there was in the big control room. The computer, they learned, was housed in another room further along the corridor, but here, as he had fervently hoped, were all the controls for the nuclear reactor. He listened with an increasing sense of urgency as the significance of each control panel was explained to them. Some of the words he was unable to follow, but he saw that Tao was taking it all in. If only these men knew that they were blithely signing their own death warrants, he reflected grimly.

The urge to give the order to dispose of

the technicians was strong within him, yet he forced himself to have patience. It was essential that they should learn as much as they could before they committed themselves to any irrevocable step. Tao questioned the others as to the orders they would receive once the satellite they intended to use as a target for the weapon came above the horizon at the exact time that the weapon was to be tested. Each question was answered without any hesitation. Obviously the others had no suspicions whatsoever. Carradine waited until Tao finally nodded and moved towards a desk. Out of the corner of his eye, he saw the other two men at the door leading into the corridor.

His fingers closed around the butt of the Luger. Slowly he drew it out and held it so as to cover all three technicians. For a moment they stared at him in surprise, as though he had suddenly gone mad.

'Stand over against the wall,' he ordered harshly.

Reluctantly they obeyed. Tao checked them for hidden weapons, then shook his head, smiling thinly.

'What is the meaning of this?' demanded one of the men tightly. 'There are guards outside and — '

'The guards are both dead,' Carradine told him tonelessly. 'Unfortunately we were forced to kill them both.'

'There are others,' said the man. He let his gaze slide from Carradine towards Tao, who had moved quickly and surely to one of the control panels and was busy flicking down a row of switches, then spinning the dials rapidly between his fingers. The look of stunned surprise on the technicians' faces changed abruptly to one of horror. The man in front of Carradine started forward, his hands outstretched as though to stop Tao. He halted abruptly as the barrel of the Luger was thrust painfully into his chest.

'You fools!' His voice rose swiftly to a high-pitched scream. Realisation must have come to him in that moment. 'If you pull out the control rods, the reaction will go out of control. There will be a chain reaction which will — '

'Which will destroy everything,' Carradine told him. There was no pity in his voice. 'Just as you intend to destroy the world with that weapon if the West refuses to bow down to you.'

He saw the look of desperation in the man's glazed eyes a split second before the other leapt forward, oblivious of the gun pressed against his ribs. Carradine's reaction was instinctive, unthinking. His fingers squeezed the trigger of its own accord. The gun slammed back against his wrist, the recoil almost breaking the bone. For a moment the technician remained upright, his grey features blank, the jaw dropping open limply. Then his legs buckled under him and he pitched forward against Carradine's knees, almost throwing him off balance. The other two technicians, on the point of jumping forward, stopped in their tracks, staring in mute horror at the body on the floor at their feet.

Tao ran back from the control panel. 'We must hurry now,' he said harshly. 'I've jammed the controls so that they won't be able to reverse the boron rods.'

'How long do we have?'

'I don't know. Minutes maybe. Possibly

half an hour. I doubt if there will be much longer.'

Carradine did not wait for any more. The thought of that ravening nuclear chaos ready to run wild only a little distance away drowned out every other thought in his mind. Before either of the technicians could make a move to defend themselves or even guess at his intentions, he had lifted the heavy Luger twice, holding it by the long barrel. The butt thudded down against their unprotected heads. He did not pause to see whether they were dead or merely unconscious. Time was of the essence now. Before their bodies had crashed to the floor he was running for the door with Tao padding silently on his heels. Out into the corridor now and hurry!

Inside the lift, Tao thumbed the topmost button. The door began to close. Hell, wouldn't it close any faster? Carradine tried to ignore the tingling in his arms and legs and the throbbing of the blood through his veins. Painfully slowly, the lift began to ascend. Standing there, his whole body tense, he realised that his nails were biting deeply, agonisingly, into the flesh of his palms. He straightened his fingers and glanced at the other men. The same thoughts were at the back of their eyes as were running through his brain. How long? Now that the restraining action of the rods had been removed and the panel smashed, there was nothing anyone could do to halt that moment of ultimate destruction.

The lift came to a halt and the door slid aside. One after the other, they tumbled out into the corridor and half-ran towards the far door. The last rays of the setting sun, just touching the topmost peaks of the distant hills, shone directly into their eyes, half-blinding them as they came out into the open. Gratefully, Carradine sucked a gust of air into his lungs.

Swiftly, he glanced about him. This was going to be a bad moment. They would have to reach the staff car in which they had come and drive out through the gate without causing suspicion. Fortunately, most of the others were still gathered around the gleaming weapon to the rear of the building. A few of the guards were visible manning the machine-gun posts around the site.

There was only bluff left to them now. Controlling the rising tide of fear in his mind, Carradine forced himself to walk slowly and unconcernedly towards the car. The urge to break into a wild run was almost more than he could fight down. But the slightest suspicious movement would result in those gates being closed and the general alarm being given. His breath harsh in his throat, Carradine opened the door of the car and slid into the seat. Tao crushed in beside him. Switching on the ignition, Tao put the vehicle into first gear and the car moved slowly towards the gates. Turning his head, Carradine threw a swift glance behind him. Through the rear window he could see one or two heads turned in their direction, but as yet no one made a move.

At the gate Tao leaned out of the window and said harshly to the waiting guard, 'We have received an urgent call to report back to Canton. The others will be staying to witness the completion of the test.'

The guard saluted and gave a brief nod of acknowledgement. Then they were out on the straight stretch of road and Tao had his foot hard down on the accelerator. The needle on the speedometer crept up swiftly. Leaning forward in his seat, Carradine scanned the road ahead for some sign of Ts'ai Luan and the others. They had left the heavy truck half a mile back on one of the narrow side roads. He fervently hoped that the others had gone back to it and would be ready to move out immediately.

★ ★ ★

They came upon the truck less than ten minutes later. Tao had driven like a crazy man once they had turned off the main road, the car jarring from side to side, threatening to skid and overturn at every corner.

Carradine had the door of the car opened before it had come to a sliding halt. Swiftly he leapt out and ran to the truck. 'Let's get out of here!' he yelled hoarsely. 'There's no time to lose. That atomic reactor back there is going to go at any minute.'

He tore the door open and climbed inside, aware of Ts'ai Luan's startled face as she helped the others into the back of the truck. Gratefully, he realised that Tai Fan had seen them coming, for the engine was already running. Good man! There was not a second wasted. Tai Fan did not even turn his head to look at him, but got the truck going. The road ahead of them twisted into a wicked S-bend, plunged down through huge boulders into a narrow valley and then began a long, twisting climb. Tai Fan took the next bend, in Carradine's estimation, much too fast, and went into a skid. But somehow even on the rough, treacherous surface he managed to come out of it.

They took the rising stretch of road at speed, the engine whining in protest. Tai Fan must have been pushing it to the absolute limit, Carradine thought. Pray God that it didn't pack in now or it would be the end for all of them. He sat tautly on the edge of the seat, aware of the sweat on his head and back. What was the radius of an atomic explosion? Two miles? Five? Maybe even as much as ten? Certainly there could be danger even outside of this critical distance. Even if they did succeed in getting outside of the area of the blast, there was still the radioactivity to take into account; that invisible, penetrating radiation that could kill just as surely as the tremendous blast.

And so the race against time went on. Tai Fan drove on the brakes and gears. But the good road was running out swiftly. They crossed a narrow bridge crossing a gaping ravine and swung around the lee of a huge overhang. On the broad dashboard, the dial to the far right gave warning that the engine was overheating badly. The needle was already hovering just above the red danger segment. Twisting in his seat, Carradine glanced into the mirror. They were high in the hills now. Maybe the great bulk of them, closing in on their tail, would prove to be a sufficient shield against the blast. Behind them, it was going dark. These hills had hidden the sun and most of the lower slopes were in deep shadow. For a moment he thought of those men back there, doomed and unknowing men except for the two technicians who might still possibly be alive. His mind seemed oddly detached. Once again he could see in his mind's eye that wide, gleaming chamber below the ground with the white tiled walls and the rows of glittering dials all around, and the nuclear reactor a short distance away, building up to the explosion point while the high-ranking officers stood around outside waiting for a tiny, gleaming star to climb above the eastern horizon and travel slowly and with a silent majesty across the clear sky, lit by the light of the setting sun and . . .

The sky behind them was suddenly lit as though by a second sun. Carradine saw the glare in the side mirror and shut his eyes instinctively. Boiling hundreds of feet into the evening sky, the glowing fireball surged upward, partly hidden by the hills as the tremendous detonation obliterated the laboratory site, tearing a great radio-active crater in the ground of the valley.

Some moments later the blast and shock waves, staggering even at that distance and reflected by the hills, reached them. The truck swayed and slid sideways for almost ten yards, threatening to go over onto its side. Tai Fan fought desperately with the spinning wheel, grasping it in his huge hands, wrestling it with all of the strength in his arms. There was a look of shock and numbed surprise on his face. Desperately, he braked. Carradine flung out a hand, grabbed hold of the window ledge, and held on until his fingers were numb with the pressure he was exerting. The thunder-clap of the explosion was so loud that the eardrums only heard it for a second and then refused to register it any longer. The blast of air swept along the road, funnelled by the hills on either side. When things finally righted themselves, Carradine sat stunned for a long moment, scarcely able to comprehend the fact that they were still alive. Slowly, he lifted his head and unhooked his fingers from the window. Tai Fan stared at him dazedly, his face muscles slack with shock.

Opening the door, Carradine stepped down, holding on to the side of the truck as his legs shook like those of a sick man, his knees bending of their own accord. Swaying, he made his way to the back of the truck. The girl's face stared at him, lips parted, eyes wide.

'That's the end of them,' he said dully. His ears popped painfully and his voice seemed to come from a far distance, droning strangely inside his head as the vibrations were carried through the bones of his skull to his brain rather than heard through his ears.

The girl, he saw, was not looking directly at him, but over his shoulder. He turned slowly, eyes narrowed. A quiver of fear bit deeply at his stomach and he felt on the point of vomiting. The terrible shape of that familiar mushroom cloud dominated the scene. Boiling outward as though in slow motion, it climbed high into the evening heavens, awe-inspiring and frightening.

'Oh God,' he muttered and it was more of a prayer than an oath. The girl leaned forward a little. Her hand fumbled for his and she held it tightly. He saw that her lower lip was trembling; that she seemed on the point of losing that tremendous self-control which had brought her through so much these past few days. He squeezed her hand and forced a weak smile. 'Try to forget it if you can,' he said. 'There was nothing else that could be done. At least they all died without knowing anything.' He did not add that they were the men who had been wanting to dominate all of China and eventually the whole of the free world.

As he made his way back to the front of the truck and swung himself up beside Tai Fan, he knew that this moment was something he would never forget. He had been forced to do a lot of dirty things in his career simply because the people he was dedicated to fighting employed the same kind of tactics and one could not fight them with kid gloves. But this was altogether different. Maybe someday in the future, he consoled himself, he would be able to look back on this day and convince himself that what he had done had been for the best, for the good of mankind as a whole. But at that particular moment, all he wanted to do was crawl away somewhere in the rocks, ask God to forgive him, and be violently sick.

★ ★ ★

In the cold and grey light of dawn, the coast looked depressing. There was a thick sea mist curling around the out-thrusting headland, obscuring most of the sea. Carradine could hear it booming on the beach some distance below, although he could scarcely see it. Ten feet away he could just make out the narrow trail, little more than an animal track which led down the cliffs to the narrow stretch of beach. Ts'ai Luan had gone down fifteen minutes before, telling him to stay there until she got back. He had wanted to go with the girl in case of trouble, but she had told him there was little danger.

One thing however; once they had reached the tiny village some three miles to the north Canton — they had taken side roads to avoid driving through the city — he had insisted that the girl should accompany him and Chao Lin to Hong Kong, overruling her protests that now their work was finished it was her duty to remain in China to gather further vital information for transmission to London whenever the opportunity arose.

He made his way slowly back to where Chao Lin sat with his back resting against the dripping rocks. The other said softly: 'You are still thinking of what happened, Mr. Carradine? If you will take the advice of an old man, put it out of your head. You did only what you had to do. If you had not succeeded, the possible consequences could have been disastrous for the world. The lives of a score of men are nothing compared with the millions that may have been slaughtered if Kao Fi Min's weapon had proved a success. Now, with his death and the destruction not only of the weapon itself, but of the papers and designs, it will take them many years to construct another.'

'I suppose you're right, Chao Lin.' Carradine gave a brief nod. He rubbed his shoulders where they had been battered and bruised during the long drive down through the hills and out to the almost deserted village where he had said farewell to Tai Fan and the others.

'I know I am right. Power is a good thing provided that it rests in the hands of the right people. In the wrong hands it can be a double-edged weapon, a sort which cuts the man who wields it as well as the victim.'

There was a faint sound behind them. Carradine turned swiftly, his hand dropping towards his gun, eyes peering into the writhing tendrils of the sea mist which swirled about him. A moment later, a rock bounced down the slope and then Ts'ai Luan materialised out of the mist. She nodded her head as Carradine glanced at her with an expression of mute interrogation. 'The boat is still there,' she said breathlessly. 'Even if anyone saw it these past two days they will not have worried overmuch. There are usually a lot of them off the coast, fishing or diving.'

'Then let's get down to it,' he said sharply. 'I won't feel safe until we reach Hong Kong.' He went over to Chao Lin. 'You'll never make it down that cliff in your condition,' he said quietly. 'I'll carry you down.'

'The path is very treacherous,' said the girl. 'You must stay very close to me and watch where I put my feet. The slightest wrong move could send you to the bottom.'

Carefully, Carradine hoisted the older man across his shoulders in a fireman's lift, then followed the girl down the dangerously narrow path. It seemed a lifetime since he had climbed it with her only a few short days before. Now in the mist clinging coldly about him, the journey was even more of a nightmare than previously. In front of him Ts'ai Luan was a vaguely seen shape, sometimes vanishing almost completely as a trick of the wind thickened the wall of mist between them.

After what seemed an eternity, he saw the pale stretch of sand below him. Then they had reached the tiny boat moored on the sand. Gently he lowered Chao Lin into it, then climbed on board. Without a word the girl took the oars and they pulled away from the cliffs, heading out into the greyness which lay over the swelling ocean.

'Are you sure you can find the junk?' he

asked after a few moments.

'I think so. It should be anchored around here somewhere.' She rested on the oars and they listened intently. For a moment Carradine could hear nothing but the muted sound of the surf on the rocks and the gentle slap of the waves against the side of the boat as it bobbed up and down in the swell. Then, from somewhere to starboard, he managed to pick out another sound, the faint grinding of metal on wood.

'The anchor chain running against the hull of the junk,' said the girl in a faint whisper. 'It must be.' She reached for the oars and pulled strongly, turning the boat. A minute later the looming bulk of the junk materialised out of the fog.

The voyage back across the channel was uneventful. Shivering in the cold air, Carradine sat with his back to the thick mast, knees drawn up to his chest, and left the sailing of the junk to the girl. Only the steady flap of the sea disturbed his thoughts. Now that they were virtually safe and there was the chance to think clearly and logically, he struggled with the clouds of nightmare that were still strong in his mind.

By now, he thought, the entire world would know that another atomic detonation had taken place inside China. The army of delicate recording instruments would have picked up the blasts and pinpointed the origin. He half-smiled at the reactions of the scientists and politicians when they finally realised just where the explosion had occurred. There would be a lot of speculation in high places in London and Washington, and possibly some guarded statements inside the Soviet Union. He could imagine the look on the Chief's face when he finally got the news through to him.

★ ★ ★

It was late the following evening. Beyond the barrier, on the tarmac, the plane for London stood gleaming in the sunlight. Already the first of the passengers were making their way out to it. Carradine had bought himself a ticket shortly after midday, had his passport examined and stamped by a keen-eyed official who had looked at him closely, then handed it back to him with a flourish. He had half-anticipated questions being asked, but there had been nothing like that.

Now there were only a few minutes left. Ts'ai Luan slipped her hand into his. 'I suppose you do have to go back so soon,' she said, a note of pleading in her voice. Tears, which he had never seen before, shone in her eyes.

'I'm afraid so.' He wanted to take her in his arms and tell her that he would only be gone for a little while; that he would come back to her and things would be as they had been. But he knew that it would be a lie, and she would know it too.

With a half-angry movement she wiped the tears away with her hand, then lifted her face to his. He bent and kissed her hungrily, hard, not wanting to let her go. Then the tannoy crackled, the impersonal voice informing everyone that the plane for London was waiting and all passengers should now make their way on board.

He suddenly knew that he would never

know another girl like this — beautiful, courageous, so full of life and vitality. Hell! Why did life always have to be so complicated; why did friendships have to last for just a little while and then come to such an abrupt end?

'You'd better go now, Steve,' she said in a voice that trembled. 'Or I shall make a fool of myself in front of everyone.' She pushed him away from her. Pushing open the gate, he walked through towards the waiting plane. As he reached it, he turned and glanced back. She was still standing there, a slight, forlorn figure, one hand raised in farewell.

He lifted his own hand, then climbed up the steps and into the plane. The stewardess gave him an odd look and a quick smile as he brushed past. Three minutes later, the engines roared and they began to move slowly towards the end of the runway. With the safety belt tightly against his stomach, he stared straight ahead of him, aware of the stinging in his own eyes. The plane paused and the pitch of the engines changed, growing into a shrill whine. Then they were racing down the wide concrete river of the runway, the ground flashing beneath the wings. The ground fell away slowly as they lifted and began to climb. Down below, the blue expanse of the South China Sea came into view with the island of Hong Kong lying placidly in the calm water.

With a tremendous effort he forced himself to relax, to forget. Almost of their own volition, his hands reached down and loosened the safety belt, allowing it to fall away from his body. The plane banked steeply. They turned into the red sunglow on the first leg of the journey back across the world.

THE END

We do hope that you have enjoyed reading this large print book.

Did you know that all of our titles are available for purchase?

We publish a wide range of high quality large print books including:
Romances, Mysteries, Classics
General Fiction
Non Fiction and Westerns

Special interest titles available in large print are:
The Little Oxford Dictionary
Music Book, Song Book
Hymn Book, Service Book

Also available from us courtesy of Oxford University Press:
Young Readers' Dictionary
(large print edition)
Young Readers' Thesaurus
(large print edition)

For further information or a free brochure, please contact us at:
Ulverscroft Large Print Books Ltd.,
The Green, Bradgate Road, Anstey,
Leicester, LE7 7FU, England.
Tel: (00 44) 0116 236 4325
Fax: (00 44) 0116 234 0205

Other titles in the
Linford Mystery Library:

STORM EVIL

John Robb

A terrible storm sweeps across a vast desert of North Africa. Five legionnaires and a captain on a training course are caught in it and take refuge in a ruined temple. Into the temple, too, come four Arabs laden with hate for the Legion captain. Then a beautiful aviator arrives — the estranged wife of the officer. When darkness falls, and the storm rages outside, the Arabs take a slow and terrible vengeance against the captain. Death strikes suddenly, often, and in a grotesque form . . .

ROOKIE COP

Richard A. Lupoff

America, June 1940. Nick Train has given up his dreams of a boxing championship after a brief and unsuccessful career in the ring. When one of his pals takes the examination for the police academy, Nick decides to join him. But what started out as a whim turns into a dangerous challenge, as Nick plays a precarious double game of collector for the mob and mole for a shadowy enforcement body ... Will the rookie cop's luck hold?

THE DEVIL'S DANCE

V. J. Banis

When Chris leaves New York for a vacation with her half-sister Pam, who is staying at a Tennessee country mansion, she discovers that the remote backwater is the site of a centuries-old feud raging between the Andrewses and the Melungeons; and Chris's elderly host, Mrs. Andrews, lives in fear. Danger lurks everywhere, from the deceptively tranquil countryside to the darkly handsome, yet mysterious, Gabe who hides amid the shadows. And when events take a more sinister turn, it seems that the curse of the Melungeons is hungry for more victims . . .